THE
King
IS COMING

An Outline Study of the Last Days

H. L. WILLMINGTON

With a foreword by Jerry Falwell

TYNDALE HOUSE PUBLISHERS
Wheaton, Illinois

Library of Congress Catalog Card Number 73-81006
ISBN 8423-2085-7 cloth; 8423-2086-5 paper

Copyright © 1973 by Tyndale House Publishers,
Wheaton, Illinois

Sixth printing, December 1977

Printed in the United States of America

CONTENTS

This book is lovingly dedicated to my wife, Sue, and my son, Matthew.

FOREWORD

Harold Willmington, outstanding Bible teacher,
is greatly loved by the students of Lynchburg Baptist
College and the Thomas Road Bible Institute, of which
he is the dean. I, too, have benefited much from his
written and spoken ministry of God's Word, and many
of my radio programs are supported by information
compiled at my request by this capable and devoted
scholar.

If Mr. Willmington has one talent which stands out
above the many others, it is his remarkable ability
to take profound truths from Scripture and simplify them
so that every listener fully understands. This textbook
is a prime example of this ability, for here we have
a succinct yet detailed summary of what the Bible
teaches about the events of "the last days" — what the
Word of God calls the blessed hope of the return of
the Lord Jesus Christ.

The doctrinal position of this book is that the rapture
of the Church will be premillenial and pretribulational.
No doctrine in the Word provides a greater incentive
for witnessing and soul-winning than that of the imminent
return of Christ, as it is outlined in *The King Is Coming*.
May we who "love his appearing" be inspired and
stimulated to wait, watch, and work as never before.

Jerry Falwell, *Pastor*
Thomas Road Baptist Church

INTRODUCTION

In 1960 I managed my father's Christian book store
in Quincy, Illinois. Often a new Christian would walk
into the store and ask for a book on prophecy.
He was just saved, he had heard that Jesus is coming soon,
he was excited, and he wanted to know more details
concerning all this. I must confess that as I led him
back to the shelf of prophecy books I would experience
both gladness and frustration — gladness because
of his intense interest, but frustration because there were
more than thirty books lined up there! Which one
would be best? Could he afford several? Even if he
could afford them, would he have time to read them?

Partly as a result of this dilemma, I began to feel
that God was leading me to become a "Reader's Digest"
theologian for his glory! The result was that I read
those thirty volumes and browsed through a good
number of others besides. I then carefully searched out
the great prophetic passages in both the Old and
New Testaments and made my own notes.

The King Is Coming is the fruit of those many hours
of research. I have not attempted to set forth any
new discoveries or revelations, but rather to review that
which has already been said — and to do it in one com-
pact volume. I have freely stood on the shoulders
of such giants as Blackstone, Ironside, Criswell, Seiss,
and other godly and gifted men. This book is intended
to be a concise but complete, nontechnical textbook
on "the last days," and is offered to the public with

these words of John in mind: "The testimony of Jesus is the spirit of prophecy" (Revelation 19:10).

H. L. Willmington
Lynchburg, Virginia

I. THE RAPTURE OF THE CHURCH

A. The Meaning of the Word "Rapture"

The term is derived from the Latin verb *rapere,* which means "to transport from one place to another." Thus the next great scheduled event predicted by the Bible will take place when the Lord Jesus comes in the air to catch up his own. Several key passages bring this out:

"For this we say to you by the word of the Lord, that we who are alive, and remain until the coming of the Lord, shall not precede those who have fallen asleep. For the Lord Himself will descend from heaven with a shout, with the voice of the archangel, and with the trumpet of God; and the dead in Christ shall rise first. Then we who are alive and remain shall be caught up together with them in the clouds to meet the Lord in the air, and thus we shall always be with the Lord" (1 Thess. 4:15-17, New American Standard Bible).

"Behold, I shew you a mystery; we shall not all sleep, but we shall all be changed, in a moment, in the twinkling of an eye, at the last trump: for the trumpet shall sound, and the dead shall be raised incorruptible, and we shall be changed. For this corruptible must put on incorruption, and this mortal must put on immortality" (1 Cor. 15:51-53).

B. The Participants of the Rapture

For whom will Jesus come? It is the view of this theological summary that Christ will come again for his church, which is composed of all saved people from Pentecost

up to the Rapture itself. The actual participants
of the Rapture include:

1. The Lord Jesus himself;

2. The archangel (perhaps Michael; see Dan. 10:
13, 21; 12:1; Jude 9; Rev. 12:7);

3. The bodies of dead believers: "for this
corruptible must put on incorruption";

4. The translated bodies of living believers:
"and this mortal must put on immortality."

C. The False Views of the Rapture

1. That the Rapture is the same as the second
coming of Christ. False! At the Rapture
Jesus comes for his church in the air, while at the
second coming he comes with his people to the earth.
See Jude 14, 15; Revelation 19:11-16.

2. That the Rapture will include only "spiritual"
Christians, and that carnal Christians will be
left behind to endure the Tribulation. This theory
is refuted by one little word in 1 Corinthians 15:51,
where Paul says that "we shall *all* be changed."
This false view is often called the "partial Rapture"
theory.

3. That the Rapture will not occur until the middle
of the Tribulation, thus forcing the entire church
to go through the first three and a half years of
God's wrath. This theory is called mid-tribulationism,
and is refuted by Paul in 1 Thessalonians 5:9,

where he says, "For God hath not appointed us to wrath. . . ."

4. That the Rapture will not occur until the end of the Tribulation. This is known as post-tribulationism, and is refuted by 1 Thessalonians 5:9 and Revelation 3:10.

The New Testament pictures the church as the body and bride of Christ. If the mid-tribulation or post-tribulation view were correct, then a part of this body would suffer amputation, and a section of the bride would be left behind! In addition to this, one would be forced to conclude that all bodies of carnal departed Christians would likewise be left in the grave. This simply is not the clear teaching of the Word of God!

The Bible teaches clearly that the Rapture is pre-tribulational in nature and includes all believers. See 1 Thessalonians 1:10 and Romans 5:9. Perhaps the strongest proof of this statement is the fact that up to chapter 6 of Revelation the church is mentioned many times, but from chapter 6 to chapter 19 (the period of the Tribulation) there is no mention whatsoever of the church on earth. In fact, the only godly group which Satan can find to persecute is the nation Israel! See Revelation chapter 12.

In Revelation 4:1 John declares, "After this I looked, and, behold, a door was opened in heaven: and the first voice which I heard was as it were of a trumpet talking with me; which said, Come up hither. . . ." We are told that Christians are God's ambassadors on earth (2 Cor. 5:20) and that he will someday declare war on this earth. The first thing a king or president does after he declares war on another country is to call

his ambassadors home! Thus we conclude that the
church will escape the Tribulation!

D. The Purpose of the Rapture

1. To judge and reward the church of God

"For we must all appear before the judgment
seat of Christ; that everyone may receive the things
done in his body . . . whether it be good or bad"
(2 Cor. 5:10).

2. To remove the Spirit of God

"For the mystery of lawlessness is already at work;
only he who now restrains will do so until he is
taken out of the way" (2 Thess. 2:7, NASB).
Many theologians believe the "he" in this verse
is a reference to the Holy Spirit. Thus the Spirit
of God has been acting as a divine dam, faithfully
holding back the waters of sin. But at the Rapture
his blessed influence will be removed to a large
extent in order to prepare the way for the
Tribulation.

E. The Mystery of the Rapture

In 1 Corinthians 15:51 Paul declares, "Behold, I show
you a mystery. . . ." What is this secret of the Savior?
Let us suppose you began reading the Bible in Genesis
chapter 1, and read through 1 Corinthians chapter 14.
If you stopped your reading here, you would already
have learned about many important facts, such as
creation, man's sin, the flood, Bethlehem, Calvary,
the resurrection, and of the existence of heaven and hell.

But you would be forced to conclude that a Christian could get to heaven only after physically dying. You would of course note the two exceptions of Enoch (Gen. 5:24) and Elijah (2 Kings 2:11), but apart from these it would be clear that believers have to travel the path of the grave to reach the goal of glory.

But now the secret is out, and here it is: Millions of Christians will someday reach heaven without dying! "Behold, I show you a mystery; we shall not all sleep, but we shall all be changed" (1 Cor. 15:51). This, then, is the mystery of the Rapture!

F. The Trumpet of the Rapture

In at least three biblical passages concerning the Rapture, a trumpet is mentioned (1 Cor. 15:52; 1 Thess. 4:16; Rev. 4:1). How are we to understand this? Dr. J. Dwight Pentecost writes, "The phrase 'the trump of God' is significant, for in the Old Testament the trumpet was used for two things — to summon to battle and to summon to worship."[1]

Which of the two meanings, however, is involved at the Rapture? Dr. Pentecost suggests that *both* meanings are in mind, one directed toward angels and the other to believers.

1. To angels the trumpet blast will mean "Prepare for battle!"

According to various New Testament passages (Eph. 6:12; John 14:30; 1 John 5:19) this present world lies in the hands of the evil one, the devil, and the very atmosphere is filled with his wicked

---

[1] J. Dwight Pentecost, *Prophecy for Today* (Grand Rapids: Zondervan), p. 30. Used by permission.

power and presence. Satan will obviously resist
believers being caught up through his domain
and becoming freed from his wicked worldly
system. Therefore, the trumpet commands the
angels, "Prepare for battle! Clear the way for
the catching up of those resurrected bodies
and those living believers!"

2. To all believers the trumpet blast will mean
"Prepare to worship!"

In Numbers 10:1-3 we read, "And the Lord spake
unto Moses, saying, 'Make thee two trumpets
of silver . . . that thou mayest use them for the
calling of the assembly . . . and when they shall
blow with them, all the assembly shall assemble
themselves to thee at the door of the
tabernacle. . . .' "

Regarding the Rapture trumpet, Numbers 10:4
seems to be especially significant: "If they blow
but with one trumpet, then the princes, which are
heads of the thousands of Israel, shall gather
themselves unto thee." At the Rapture only one
trumpet is sounded, suggesting that in God's sight
all believers occupy a place of utmost importance!
We are all "head princes" in the mind of God.

G. The Old Testament Foreshadowing of the Rapture

1. Seen in Enoch, who was taken from the world
before the flood judgment (Gen. 5:24).

2. Seen in Lot, who was removed from Sodom
before the fire judgment (Gen. 19:22-24).

H. *The Challenge of the Rapture*

Because of this glorious coming event the child of God
is instructed to do many things.

1. He is to attend the services of the Lord
regularly.

". . . not forsaking the assembling of ourselves
together, as the manner of some is; but exhorting
one another; and so much the more, as ye see the
day approaching" (Heb. 10:25).

2. He is to observe the Lord's Supper with the
Rapture in mind.

"For as often as ye eat this bread, and drink this cup,
ye do show the Lord's death till he come"
(1 Cor. 11:26).

3. He is to love believers and all men.

"And the Lord make you to increase and abound
in love one toward another, and toward all men . . .
to the end he may stablish your hearts . . . at
the coming of our Lord Jesus Christ with all his
saints" (1 Thess. 3:12, 13).

4. He is to be patient.

"Be ye also patient; stablish your hearts; for the
coming of the Lord draweth nigh" (James 5:8).

5. He is to live a separated life.

". . . we know that, when he shall appear,
we shall be like him, for we shall see him as he is.
And every man that hath this hope in him
purifieth himself . . ." (1 John 3:2, 3).
". . . denying ungodliness and worldly lusts, we

should live soberly, righteously, and godly, in this
present world; looking for that blessed hope,
and the glorious appearing of the great God and
our Saviour Jesus Christ" (Titus 2:12, 13).
"And now, little children, abide in him, that,
when he shall appear, we may have confidence,
and not be ashamed before him at his coming"
(1 John 2:28).

6. He is to refrain from judging others.

"Therefore judge nothing before the time, until the
Lord come, who both will bring to light the
hidden things of darkness, and will make manifest
the counsels of the hearts; and then shall every man
have praise of God" (1 Cor. 4:5).

7. He is to preach the Word.

"I charge thee therefore before God, and the
Lord Jesus Christ, who shall judge the quick and
the dead at his appearing and his kingdom;
preach the word . . ." (2 Tim. 4:1, 2).
"Feed the flock of God . . . and when the chief
Shepherd shall appear, ye shall receive a crown of
glory that fadeth not away" (1 Peter 5:2, 4).

8. He is to comfort the bereaved.

"For the Lord himself shall descend from heaven
. . . wherefore comfort one another with these
words" (1 Thess. 4:16, 18).

9. He is to win souls.

"Keep yourselves in the love of God, looking for
the mercy of our Lord Jesus Christ unto eternal life.
And of some have compassion, making a

difference: and others save with fear, pulling them out of the fire . . ." (Jude 21-23).

10. He is to be concerned with heaven.

"If ye then be risen with Christ, seek those things which are above, where Christ sitteth on the right hand of God. Set your affection on things above, not on things on the earth. For ye are dead, and your life is hid with Christ in God. When Christ, who is our life, shall appear, then shall ye also appear with him in glory" (Col. 3:1-4).

I. The Effect of the Rapture

What will be the reaction of a sin-sick society when millions of people suddenly disappear? In his well-known book *The Late Great Planet Earth,* Hal Lindsey writes:

"There I was, driving down the freeway and all of a sudden the place went crazy . . . cars going in all directions . . . and not one of them had a driver. I mean it was wild! I think we've got an invasion from outer space!"

"It was the last quarter of the championship game and the other side was ahead. Our boys had the ball. We made a touchdown and tied it up. The crowd went crazy. Only one minute to go and they fumbled — our quarterback recovered — he was about a yard from the goal when — zap — no more quarterback — completely gone, just like that!"

"It was puzzling — very puzzling. I was teaching my course in the Philosophy of Religion when all of a sudden three of my students vanished. They simply vanished! They were quite argumentative — always trying to prove their point from the Bible. No great loss to the class. However, I do find this disappearance very difficult to explain."

"As an official spokesman for the United Nations I wish to inform all peace-loving people of the world that we are making every human effort to assist those nations whose leaders have disappeared. We have issued a general declaration of condemnation in the General Assembly concerning these heads of state. Their irresponsibility is shocking."

"My dear friends in the congregation. Bless you for coming to church today. I know that many of you have lost loved ones in this unusual disappearance of so many people. However, I believe that God's judgment has come upon them for their continued dissension and quarreling with the great advances of the church in our century. Now that the reactionaries are removed, we can progress toward our great and glorious goal of uniting all mankind into a brotherhood of reconciliation and understanding."

"You really want to know what I think? I think all that talk about the Rapture and going to meet Jesus Christ in the air wasn't crazy after all. I don't know about you, brother, but I'm going to find myself a Bible and read all those verses my wife underlined. I wouldn't listen to her while she was here, and now she's — I don't know where she is."[2]

Certainly the believers will be missed! It is evident from the Bible that the sudden disappearance of both Enoch and Elijah (two Old Testament types of the

---

[2]Hal Lindsey, *The Late Great Planet Earth* (Grand Rapids: Zondervan). Used by permission.

Rapture) caused considerable confusion and alarm among their friends.

"By faith Enoch was translated that he should not see death; and was not found, because God had translated him" (Heb. 11:5).

Especially interesting are the words, "and was not found." Enoch was doubtless the object of a great manhunt!

The Scriptures describe the later translation of Elijah in even greater detail, as the citizens of Jericho ask Elisha about the disappearance of his master:

" 'Sir,' they said, 'just say the word and fifty of our best athletes will search the wilderness for your master; perhaps the Spirit of the Lord has left him on some mountain or in some ravine.' 'No,' Elisha said, 'don't bother.' But they kept urging until he was embarrassed, and finally said, 'All right, go ahead.' Then fifty men searched for three days, but didn't find him" (2 Kings 2:16, 17, *The Living Bible*).

How much more confusion and alarm will come from the sudden and mysterious disappearance of literally millions of men and women, boys and girls!

II. THE "BEMA"– THE JUDGMENT SEAT OF CHRIST

A. The Meaning of the Bema Judgment

The Greek word *bema* (translated "judgment seat"
in the KJV) was a familiar term to the people of Paul's
day. Dr. Lehman Strauss writes:

"In the large olympic arenas, there was an elevated seat
on which the judge of the contest sat. After the contests
were over, the successful competitors would assemble
before the bema to receive their rewards or crowns.
The bema was not a judicial bench where someone
was condemned; it was a reward seat. Likewise,
the Judgment Seat of Christ is not a judicial bench . . . the
Christian life is a race, and the divine umpire is watching
every contestant. After the church has run her course,
He will gather every member before the bema
for the purpose of examining each one and giving
the proper reward to each."[3]

B. The Fact of the Bema Judgment

Many New Testament verses speak of this.

"But why dost thou judge thy brother? Or why dost
thou set at nought thy brother? For we shall all stand
before the judgment seat of Christ. For it is written,
As I live, saith the Lord, every knee shall bow to me,
and every tongue shall confess to God. So then
every one of us shall give account of himself to God"
(Rom. 14:10-12).

---

[3]Lehman Strauss, *God's Plan for the Future* (Grand Rapids: Zondervan),
p. 111. Used by permission.

"Every man's work shall be made manifest, for the day shall declare it . . ." (1 Cor. 3:13).
"For we must all appear before the judgment seat of Christ . . ." (2 Cor. 5:10).

C. The Purpose of the Bema Judgment

1. Negative considerations

a. The purpose of the Bema Judgment is *not* to determine whether a particular individual enters heaven or not, for every man's eternal destiny is already determined before he leaves this life.

b. The purpose of the Bema Judgment is *not* to punish believers for sins committed either before or after their salvation. The Scriptures are very clear that no child of God will have to answer for his sins after this life.

"He hath not dealt with us after our sins, nor rewarded us according to our iniquities.
"For as the heaven is high above the earth, so great is his mercy toward them that fear him.
"As far as the east is from the west, so far hath he removed our transgressions from us" (Psa. 103:10-12).
"Thou hast in love to my soul delivered it from the pit of corruption: for thou hast cast all my sins behind thy back" (Isa. 38:17).
"I have blotted out . . . thy transgressions and . . . thy sins" (Isa. 44:22).

"Thou wilt cast all their sins into the depths
of the sea" (Mic. 7:19).
"For I will be merciful . . . and their sins and
their iniquities will I remember no more"
(Heb. 8:12).
"The blood of Jesus Christ his Son cleanseth us
from all sin" (1 John 1:7).

2.   Positive considerations

What then is the purpose of the Bema Judgment?
In 1 Corinthians 4:2 Paul says that all Christians
should conduct themselves as faithful stewards of
God: "Moreover it is required in stewards,
that a man be found faithful."

The Apostle Peter later writes in a similar way:
"Minister . . . as good stewards of the manifold
grace of God" (1 Pet. 4:10).

In the New Testament world, a steward was the
manager of a large household or estate. He was
appointed by the owner and was entrusted
to keep the estate running smoothly. He had the
power to hire and fire and to spend and save,
being answerable to the owner alone. His only
concern was that periodic meeting with his master,
at which time he was required to account for the
condition of the estate up to that point.

With this background in mind, it may be said
that someday at the Bema Judgment all stewards will
stand before their Lord and Master and be
required to give an account of the way
they have used their privileges and responsibilities
from the moment of their conversion.
In conclusion, it can be seen that:

a. In the past, God dealt with us as sinners
(Eph. 2:1-3; 1 Cor. 6:9-11; Rom. 5:6-8).

b. In the present, God deals with us as sons
(Rom. 8:14; Heb. 12:5-11; 1 John 3:1, 2).

c. In the future, God will deal with us
(at the Bema) as stewards.

D. The Materials to be Tested at the Bema Judgment

In 1 Corinthians 3:11 the Apostle Paul explains
the glorious fact that at the moment of salvation a
repenting sinner is firmly placed on the foundation of
the death, burial, and resurrection of Christ himself!
His continuing instruction after his salvation is to rise up
and build upon this foundation.

Paul says, "But let every man take heed how he buildeth
thereupon. . . . Now if any man build upon this
foundation gold, silver, precious stones, wood, hay,
stubble, every man's work shall be made manifest,
for the day shall declare it, because it shall be revealed
by fire; and the fire shall try every man's work of what
sort it is" (1 Cor. 3:10, 12, 13).

1. Negative considerations

It should be noted immediately that this passage
does *not* teach the false doctrine known
as purgatory, for it is the believer's *works* and not
the believer *himself* that will be subjected to the fires!

2. Positive considerations

From these verses it is apparent that God classifies
the works of believers into one of the following
six areas: gold, silver, precious stones, wood,

hay, stubble. There has been much speculation
about the kinds of work down here that will
constitute gold or silver up there. But it seems
more appropriate to note that the six objects can be
readily placed into two categories:

> a. Those indestructible and worthy objects
> which will survive and thrive in the fires.
> These are the gold, silver, and precious stones.

> b. Those destructible and worthless objects
> which will be totally consumed in the fires.
> These are the wood, hay, and stubble.

Though it is difficult to know just what goes to make up
a "golden work" or a "stubble work," we are
nevertheless informed of certain general areas in
which God is particularly interested.

1. How we treat other believers

"For God is not unrighteous to forget your work
and labour of love, which ye have showed
toward his name, in that ye have ministered to
the saints, and do minister" (Heb. 6:10).
"He that receiveth a prophet in the name of a
prophet shall receive a prophet's reward;
and he that receiveth a righteous man in the name
of a righteous man shall receive a righteous man's
reward. And whosoever shall give to drink
unto one of these little ones a cup of cold water
only in the name of a disciple, verily I say unto you,
he shall in no wise lose his reward"
(Matt. 10:41, 42).

2. How we exercise our authority over others

"Obey them that have the rule over you, and submit

yourselves: for they watch for your souls, as they
that must give account, that they may do it with joy,
and not with grief . . ." (Heb. 13:17).
"Let not many of you become teachers,
my brethren, knowing that as such we shall incur
a stricter judgment" (James 3:1, NASB).

3. How we employ our God-given abilities

"Wherefore I put thee in remembrance that thou
stir up the gift of God which is in thee . . ."
(2 Tim. 1:6).
"Now there are varieties of gifts, but the same
Spirit . . . But one and the same Spirit
works all these things, distributing to each one
individually just as He wills" (1 Cor. 12:4, 11,
NASB).
"As each one has received a special gift,
employ it in serving one another, as good stewards
of the manifold grace of God" (1 Peter 4:10, NASB).

To these verses can be added the overall teaching
of Jesus' parables of the ten pounds (Luke 19:11-26)
and the eight talents (Matt. 25:14-29).

4. How we use our money

"Charge them that are rich in this world
that they be not highminded, nor trust in uncertain
riches, but in the living God, who giveth us richly
all things to enjoy; that they do good, that they be
rich in good works, ready to distribute,
willing to communicate, laying up in store for
themselves a good foundation against the time to
come, that they may lay hold on eternal life"
(1 Tim. 6:17-19).
"But this I say, He which soweth sparingly

shall reap also sparingly; and he which soweth
bountifully shall reap also bountifully. Every man
according as he purposeth in his heart,
so let him give; not grudgingly, or of necessity,
for God loveth a cheerful giver" (2 Cor. 9:6, 7).
"Upon the first day of the week let every one of you
lay by him in store, as God hath prospered him . . ."
(1 Cor. 16:2).

5. How much we suffer for Jesus

"Blessed are ye, when men shall revile you,
and persecute you, and shall say all maner of evil
against you falsely, for my sake. Rejoice, and be
exceeding glad, for great is your reward in
heaven . . ." (Matt. 5:11, 12).
"Beloved, think it not strange concerning
the fiery trial which is to try you, as though some
strange thing happened unto you; but rejoice,
inasmuch as ye are partakers of Christ's sufferings,
that, when his glory shall be revealed, ye may be
glad also with exceeding joy" (1 Peter 4:12, 13).
"And Jesus answered and said, Verily I say unto you,
there is no man that hath left house, or brethren,
or sisters, or father, or mother, or wife,
or children, or lands, for my sake, and the gospel's,
but he shall receive an hundredfold now in this time,
houses, and brethren, and sisters, and mothers,
and children, and lands, with persecutions;
and in the world to come eternal life"
(Mark 10:29, 30).
"For our light affliction, which is but for a moment,
worketh for us a far more exceeding and eternal
weight of glory" (2 Cor. 4:17).
"For I reckon that the sufferings of this present time

are not worthy to be compared with the glory
which shall be revealed in us" (Rom. 8:18).

6. How we spend our time

". . . redeeming the time, because the days are evil"
(Eph. 5:16).
"Walk in wisdom . . . redeeming the time"
(Col. 4:5).
"And if ye call on the Father, who without respect
of persons judgeth according to every man's work,
pass the time of your sojourning here in fear"
(1 Peter 1:17).
"So teach us to number our days, that we may
apply our hearts unto wisdom" (Psa. 90:12).

7. How we run that particular race which God
has chosen for us

"Know ye not that they which run in a race
run all, but one receiveth the prize? So run,
that ye may obtain" (1 Cor. 9:24).
"Brethren, I count not myself to have
apprehended; but this one thing I do, forgetting
those things which are behind, and reaching forth
unto those things which are before, I press toward
the mark for the prize of the high calling of God
in Christ Jesus" (Phil. 3:13, 14).
"Let us lay aside every weight, and the sin
which doth so easily beset us, and let us run with
patience the race that is set before us"
(Heb. 12:1).
". . . that I may rejoice in the day of Christ,
that I have not run in vain . . ." (Phil. 2:16).

8. How effectively we control the old nature

"And every man that striveth for the mastery is

temperate in all things. Now they do it to obtain
a corruptible crown, but we an incorruptible.
I therefore so run, not as uncertainly; so fight I,
not as one that beateth the air. But I keep under
my body, and bring it into subjection, lest that by
any means when I have preached to others, I myself
should be a castaway" (1 Cor. 9:25-27).

9. How many souls we witness to and win to Christ

"The fruit of the righteous is a tree of life,
and he that winneth souls is wise" (Prov. 11:30).
"For what is our hope, or joy, or crown of
rejoicing? Are not even ye in the presence of
our Lord Jesus Christ at his coming? For ye are
our glory and joy" (1 Thess. 2:19, 20).
"And they that be wise shall shine as the
brightness of the firmament, and they that turn
many to righteousness as the stars for ever and ever"
(Dan. 12:3).

10. How we react to temptation

"My brethren, count it all joy when ye fall into
divers temptations, knowing this, that the trying of
your faith worketh patience" (James 1:2, 3).
"Behold, the devil shall cast some of you into prison,
that ye may be tried; and ye shall have tribulation
ten days; be thou faithful unto death, and I will
give thee a crown of life" (Rev. 2:10).

11. How much the doctrine of the Rapture means
to us

"Henceforth there is laid up for me a crown
of righteousness, which the Lord, the righteous
judge, shall give me at that day; and not to me only,

but unto all them also that love his appearing"
(2 Tim. 4:8).

12.   How faithful we are to the Word of God
and the flock of God

"Feed the flock of God which is among you,
taking the oversight thereof, not by constraint,
but willingly; not for filthy lucre, but of a ready
mind; neither as being lords over God's heritage,
but being ensamples to the flock. And when
the Chief Shepherd shall appear, ye shall
receive a crown of glory that fadeth not away"
(1 Peter 5:2-4).
"I charge thee therefore before God and the Lord
Jesus Christ, who shall judge the quick and the dead
at his appearing and his kingdom, Preach the
word . . ." (2 Tim. 4:1, 2).
"Wherefore, I take you to record this day, that I am
pure from the blood of all men. For I have
not shunned to declare unto you all the counsel
of God. Take heed therefore unto yourselves,
and to all the flock over which the Holy Ghost
hath made you overseers, to feed the church of God,
which he hath purchased with his own blood"
(Acts 20:26-28).

E. The Results of the Bema Judgment Seat of Christ

1.   Some will receive rewards.

"If any man's work abide which he hath built
thereupon, he shall receive a reward"
(1 Cor. 3:14).

The Bible mentions at least five possible rewards.

These have already been described briefly under
the last section. The rewards include:

> a. The incorruptible crown — given to those
> who master the old nature (1 Cor. 9:25-27).
>
> b. The crown of rejoicing — given to soul-
> winners (Prov. 11:30; 1 Thess. 2:19, 20;
> Dan. 12:3).
>
> c. The crown of life — given to those who
> successfully endure temptation (James 1:2, 3;
> Rev. 2:10).
>
> d. The crown of righteousness — given to
> those who especially love the doctrine of the
> Rapture (2 Tim. 4:8).
>
> e. The crown of glory — given to faithful
> preachers and teachers (1 Peter 5:2-4;
> 2 Tim. 4:1, 2; Acts 20:26-28).

It has been suggested that these "crowns" will
actually be talents and abilities with which to glorify
Christ. Thus, the greater the reward, the greater
the ability!

Who down here has not longed to be able to sing
like a George Beverly Shea or to preach like
a Billy Graham? It may be that this blessing
will be possible up there!

2. Some will suffer loss.

"If any man's work shall be burned, he shall suffer
loss . . ." (1 Cor. 3:15). This word for "suffer"
is *zemioo* in the Greek New Testament,
and is used again by Paul in Philippians chapter 3,

where he describes those things which were
the greatest source of pride to him prior to
salvation. He tells us,

"For I went through the Jewish initiation ceremony
when I was eight days old, having been born
into a pureblooded Jewish home that was a branch
of the old original Benjamin family. So I was a
real Jew if there ever was one! What's more,
I was a member of the Pharisees who demand
the strictest obedience to every Jewish law
and custom. And sincere? Yes, so much so that I
greatly persecuted the church; and I tried to obey
every Jewish rule and regulation right down to the
very last point" (Phil. 3:5, 6, TLB).

But after his conversion Paul writes, ". . . for whom
I have suffered the loss of all things . . . that I
may win Christ" (Phil. 3:8).

The point of all these teachings is simply this:
at the Bema Judgment the carnal Christian
will suffer the loss of many past achievements,
even as Paul did, but with one important exception
— Paul was richly compensated, since he suffered
his loss to win Christ, while the carnal believer
will receive nothing to replace his burned-up wood,
hay, and stubble!

Before leaving this section the question may be
asked, "Is it possible for someone who has earned
certain rewards down here to lose them somehow
through carnality?" Some believe this to be
tragically possible on the basis of the following
verses:

"Look to yourselves, that we lose not those things
which we have wrought, but that we receive
a full reward" (2 John 1:8).

"Behold, I come quickly; hold that fast which
thou hast, that no man take thy crown" (Rev. 3:11).
"Let no man beguile you of your reward . . ."
(Col. 2:18).

F. The Old Testament Foreshadowing of the Bema Judgment Seat of Christ

Although the church is nowhere mentioned
in the Old Testament, there is nevertheless a passage
which can very easily be applied to the Bema Judgment.
This can be found in the words of Boaz (a foreshadowing
of Christ) to Ruth (a foreshadowing of the church),
when he says, "It hath fully been showed me,
all that thou hast done. . . . The Lord recompense
thy work, and a full reward be given thee of the Lord
God of Israel, under whose wings thou art come to trust"
(Ruth 2:11, 12).

III. THE MARRIAGE OF THE LAMB

A. The Fact of the Marriage

Many passages in the Word of God teach that the most fantastic and wonderful wedding of all time is yet to take place in this universe.

1. This Marriage is described through the parables of Jesus.

"Let your loins be girded about, and your lights burning, and ye yourselves like unto men that wait for their Lord, when he will return from the wedding" (Luke 12:35, 36).
"The kingdom of heaven is like unto a certain king, which made a marriage for his son" (Matt. 22:2).
"Then shall the kingdom of heaven be likened unto ten virgins, which took their lamps, and went forth to meet the bridegroom" (Matt. 25:1).

2. This Marriage is described through the vision of John.

"Let us be glad and rejoice, and give honour to him; for the marriage of the Lamb is come, and his wife hath made herself ready" (Rev. 19:7).

B. The Host of the Marriage

The New Testament very clearly presents the Father as the divine host who gives this marriage. He is pictured as preparing it, then sending his servants out to invite the selected guests (Luke 14:16-23).

C. *The Bridegroom of the Marriage*

The Father's beloved Son (Matt. 3:17; 17:5), the Lord
Jesus Christ, is the bridegroom!

1. As stated by John the Baptist

"John answered and said, A man can receive
nothing except it be given him from heaven. Ye
yourselves bear me witness that I said, I am not
the Christ, but that I am sent before him. He that
hath the bride is the bridegroom; but the friend
of the bridegroom, which standeth and heareth him,
rejoiceth greatly because of the bridegroom's voice:
this my joy therefore is fulfilled. He must increase,
but I must decrease" (John 3:27-30).

2. As stated by the Lord Jesus Christ

"I came not to call the righteous, but sinners to
repentance. And they said unto him, Why do the
disciples of John fast often, and make prayers . . .
but thine eat and drink? And he said unto them,
Can ye make the children of the bridechamber
fast while the bridegroom is with them? But the
days will come when the bridegroom shall be taken
away from them, and then shall they fast in those
days" (Luke 5:32-35).

D. *The Bride of the Marriage*

In two key passages the Apostle Paul makes crystal clear
the identity of the bride:

"Wives, submit yourselves unto your own husbands,
as unto the Lord. For the husband is the head of the wife,
even as Christ is the head of the church; and he is

the Saviour of the body. Therefore, as the church
is subject unto Christ, so let the wives be to their own
husbands in everything. Husbands, love your wives,
even as Christ also loved the church, and gave himself
for it, that he might sanctify and cleanse it with the
washing of water by the Word, that he might present it
to himself a glorious church, not having spot,
or wrinkle, or any such thing; but that it should be holy
and without blemish. So ought men to love their wives
as their own bodies. He that loveth his wife loveth himself.
For no man ever yet hated his own flesh, but nourisheth
and cherisheth it, even as the Lord the church.
For we are members of his body, of his flesh, and of his
bones. For this cause shall a man leave his father
and mother, and shall be joined unto his wife,
and they two shall be one flesh. This is a great mystery;
but I speak concerning Christ and the church"
(Eph. 5:22-32).
"For I am jealous over you with godly jealousy,
for I have espoused you to one husband, that I may
present you as a chaste virgin to Christ" (2 Cor. 11:2).

E. The Guests of the Marriage

"And he saith unto me, Write, Blessed are they
which are called unto the marriage supper of the
Lamb . . ." (Rev. 19:9).

Who are these invited guests of the Lamb's Marriage
to the church?

1. In general

A group which would include all believing Gentiles
who were converted prior to Pentecost
or after the Rapture.

2. In particular

A group which would include all saved Israelites
everywhere. The ten virgins mentioned in Matthew
25 are Israelites. The five wise represent
saved Israelites and the five foolish represent
unsaved ones. They cannot represent the church,
for the church is the *bride,* inside with the
bridegroom! The virgins are guests who have been
invited to the wedding. Note that a bride is never
invited to her own wedding. If she refuses to come,
there is no wedding!

F. The Service Schedule of the Marriage

The marriage of Christ to the church will follow
the oriental pattern of marriage as described for us
in the New Testament. It consisted of three separate
stages:

1. The betrothal stage

New Testament marriages were often begun when
the couple was very young (sometimes even prior
to birth) by the groom's father. He would sign
a legal enactment before the proper judge,
pledging his son to a chosen girl. The father
would then offer the proper dowry payment.
Thus, even though the bride had never seen
the groom, she was nevertheless betrothed
or espoused to him. A New Testament example
of this first step was that of Mary and Joseph.

"Now the birth of Jesus Christ was on this wise:
when as his mother Mary was espoused to Joseph,
before they came together, she was found with child
of the Holy Ghost" (Matt. 1:18).

Both Mary and Joseph had come from Bethlehem
and had perhaps been betrothed, or promised to
each other, since childhood. But now Mary was
found to be with child before the marriage could be
consummated, and of course Joseph could arrive
at only one conclusion — she had been untrue
to him! Then the angel of the Lord explained
to Joseph the glories of the virgin birth!

Thus the betrothal stage consisted of two steps:

a. The selection of the bride

b. The payment of the dowry

With this in mind we can state that the marriage
of the Lamb is still in its betrothal stage:

a. The bride has been selected!

"Blessed be the God and Father of our
Lord Jesus Christ, who hath blessed us with all
spiritual blessings in heavenly places in Christ,
according as he hath chosen us in him
before the foundation of the world, that
we should be holy and without blame before
him in love" (Eph. 1:3, 4).

b. The dowry has been paid!

"What? Know ye not that your body is the
temple of the Holy Ghost which is in you,
which ye have of God, and ye are not your own?
For ye are bought with a price. Therefore,
glorify God in your body and in your spirit,
which are God's" (1 Cor. 6:19, 20).
"Forasmuch as ye know that ye were not
redeemed with corruptible things, as silver

and gold . . . but with the precious blood
of Christ, as of a lamb without blemish
and without spot" (1 Peter 1:18, 19).

2. The presentation stage

At the proper time the father would send
to the house of the bride servants carrying
the proper legal contract. The bride would then
be led to the home of the groom's father.

When all was ready, the father of the bride
would place her hand in the hand of the groom's
father. He would then place her hand in that
of his son.

Applying this background to the marriage of the
Lamb, the church still awaits this second phase,
the presentation stage, which we know as the
Rapture! The following verses speak of this
presentation stage:

". . . Christ also loved the church and gave himself
for it . . . that he might present it to himself
a glorious church, not having spot or wrinkle
or any such thing, but that it should be holy
and without blemish" (Eph. 5:25, 27).
"Now unto him that is able to keep you from falling,
and to present you faultless before the presence
of his glory with exceeding joy . . ." (Jude 24).
"Let us be glad and rejoice, and give honour to him,
for the marriage of the Lamb is come,
and his wife hath made herself ready. And to her
was granted that she should be arrayed in fine linen,
clean and white; for the fine linen is the
righteousness of saints" (Rev. 19:7, 8).

Then follow the events which comprise the second
stage:

a. The Heavenly Father will send for the
bride.

"After this I looked, and behold, a door was
opened in heaven; and the first voice which
I heard was as it were of a trumpet talking
with me, which said, Come up hither . . ."
(Rev. 4:1).

b. The proper legal papers of marriage
will be shown.

"Nevertheless the foundation of God
standeth sure, having this seal, the Lord
knoweth them that are his . . ." (2 Tim. 2:19).

c. The bride will be taken to the Father's
home.

"In my Father's house are many mansions;
if it were not so I would have told you.
I go to prepare a place for you. And if I go
and prepare a place for you, I will come again
and receive you unto myself, that where I am,
there ye may be also" (John 14:2, 3).

3. The celebration stage

After the private marriage service was completed
the public marriage supper would begin.
To this many guests would be invited. It was during
such a celebration that our Lord performed his first
miracle, that of changing water into wine
(see John 2:1-11). Jesus later made reference
to this third step when he spoke the following words:

"Let your loins be girded about and your lights
burning, and ye yourselves like unto men
that wait for their Lord, when he will return
from the wedding. . . . Blessed are those servants

whom the Lord, when he cometh, shall find
watching. Verily I say unto you, that he shall
gird himself and make them to sit down to meat,
and will come forth and serve them"
(Luke 12:35-37).
"Then said he unto him, A certain man made a
great supper and bade many, and sent his servant
at supper time to say to them that were bidden,
Come, for all things are now ready"
(Luke 14:16, 17).
"The kingdom of heaven is like unto a certain king,
which made a marriage for his son, and sent forth
his servants to call them that were bidden
to the wedding . . ." (Matt. 22:2, 3).

G. The Time of the Marriage

When does the wedding transpire? In view of what
has already been said, it would seem that the wedding
service (the presentation stage) will be privately
conducted in heaven, perhaps shortly after the Bema
Judgment Seat of Christ. The wedding *supper*
(the celebration stage) will be publicly conducted
on earth shortly after the second coming of Christ.

It is no accident that the Bible describes the millennium
as occurring right after the celebration supper has begun.
(The supper is described in Revelation 19 while the
millennium is described in Revelation 20.) In
New Testament times the length and cost of this supper
was determined by the wealth of the father. Therefore,
when his beloved Son is married, the Father of all grace
(whose wealth is unlimited) will rise to the occasion
by giving his Son and the bride a hallelujah celebration
which will last for a thousand years!

H. *The Old Testament Foreshadowing of the Marriage*

The 45th Psalm, written by Korah, has often been
referred to as "the Psalm of the wedding of the King."
It is reproduced here from *The Living Bible*:

> My heart is overflowing with a beautiful thought!
> I will write a lovely poem to the King, for I am
> as full of words as the speediest writer pouring out
> his story.
>
> 2You are the fairest of all;
> Your words are filled with grace;
> God himself is blessing you forever.
> 3Arm yourself, O Mighty One,
> So glorious, so majestic!
> 4And in your majesty
> Go on to victory,
> Defending truth, humility, and justice.
> Go forth to awe-inspiring deeds!
> 5Your arrows are sharp
> In your enemies' hearts;
> They fall before you.
> 6Your throne, O God, endures forever.
> Justice is your royal scepter.
> 7You love what is good
> And hate what is wrong.
> Therefore God, your God,
> Has given you more gladness
> Than anyone else.
>
> 8Your robes are perfumed with myrrh, aloes and
> cassia. In your inlaid palaces of ivory,
> lovely music is being played for your enjoyment.
> 9Kings' daughters are among your concubines.
> Standing beside you is the queen, wearing jewelry

of finest gold from Ophir. [10,11]"I advise you,
O daughter, not to fret about your parents
in your homeland far away. Your royal husband
delights in your beauty. Reverence him,
for he is your lord. [12]The people of Tyre, the
richest people of our day, will shower you
with gifts and entreat your favors."

[13]The bride, a princess, waits within her chamber,
robed in beautiful clothing woven with gold.
[14]Lovely she is, led beside her maids of honor
to the king! [15]What a joyful, glad procession
as they enter in the palace gates! [16]"Your sons
will some day be kings like their father. They shall
sit on thrones around the world!

[17]"I will cause your name to be honored in all
generations; the nations of the earth will
praise you forever."

One could almost see Korah, representing the Jerusalem
Press, being invited to that future glorious event — the
wedding of a King! He describes vividly for us the glory
of the Bridegroom (verses 2-8), the expensive wedding
gifts (verse 12), the loveliness of the bride (verses 13, 14),
and the joyful rice-throwing crowd (verse 15)!

1. The Certainty of the Marriage

Earthly marriages may be prevented because
of various unexpected problems.

> 1. In an earthly wedding there can be a
> last-minute refusal on the part of either the bride
> or groom. But not with the heavenly marriage!

> > a. The bridegroom has already expressed his

great love for his bride (Eph. 5:25),
and he never changes!

"This same Jesus, which is taken up from you
into heaven, shall so come in like manner
as ye have seen him go into heaven"
(Acts 1:11).
". . . Jesus Christ, the same yesterday,
and today, and forever" (Heb. 13:8).

b. The bride has already been glorified and
is sinless, and therefore cannot be tempted
into changing her mind or losing her love for
the Bridegroom!

"For by one offering he hath perfected forever
them that are sanctified" (Heb. 10:14).
". . . a glorious church, not having spot,
or wrinkle . . . but . . . holy and without
blemish" (Eph. 5:27).

2. In an earthly wedding a serious legal problem
might arise, such as lack of age, or even that
of a previous marriage — but not in the
heavenly wedding! (See Romans 8:33-39).

3. In an earthly wedding the tragedy of death
might intervene — but not in the heavenly
wedding!

a. The bride will never die.

"And whosoever liveth and believeth in me
shall never die" (John 11:26).

b. The Bridegroom will never die.

"I am he that liveth, and was dead; and
behold, I am alive forever more; Amen"
(Rev. 1:18).

IV. THE CRISIS OF A SEVEN-SEALED BOOK

A. The Proclamation

"And I saw in the right hand of him that sat on the throne a book written within and on the backside, sealed with seven seals. And I saw a strong angel proclaiming with a loud voice, Who is worthy to open the book, and to loose the seals thereof?" (Rev. 5:1, 2).

The circumstances surrounding this crisis occur shortly after the Rapture of the church. John has been caught up into heaven (Rev. 4:1), where he writes about the marvelous things he sees and hears.

1. He sees the glory of the Father upon the throne (Rev. 4:2, 3).

2. He sees a beautiful green rainbow around this throne (Rev. 4:3).

3. He sees twenty-four elders with golden crowns (Rev. 4:4). (These twenty-four may consist of a special representative body of both Old Testament and New Testament saints. The Greek text tells us they are all wearing *stephanos* crowns, or martyrs' crowns, rather than diadems, or monarchs' crowns. Thus they must be humans rather than angels!)

4. He hears lightnings and thunderings, which means that the awful storm of the Great Tribulation is about to unleash its fury (Rev. 4:5).

5. He sees a crystal sea of glass (Rev. 4:6).

Dr. Donald Barnhouse has written concerning this sea,

"Before the throne there was a glassy sea, like crystal. The concordance immediately takes us to the temple built by Solomon after the model of the tabernacle. 'And he made a molten sea, ten cubits from the one brim to the other; it was round all about, and its height was five cubits' (1 Kings 7:23). This great basin, fifteen feet in diameter, was supported on the backs of twelve oxen of brass, facing outward. Here the priests came for their cleansing. Each time before they entered the holy place they stopped for the cleansing ceremony.

"But thank God the laver will be turned to crystal. The day will come when none of the saints will ever need confession!

"One of the greatest joys in the anticipation of Heaven is that the laver is of crystal. I shall never have to go to the Heavenly Father again to tell Him I have sinned. I shall never have to meet that gaze of Christ that caused Peter to go out and weep bitterly. The laver is of crystal only because I and all the saints of all the ages will have been made like unto the Lord Jesus Christ."[4]

6. He sees and hears the testimony of four special angelic creatures (Rev. 4:6-8).

The first of these creatures had the characteristics of a lion, the second of a calf, the third of a man, and the fourth of an eagle. These six things John sees and writes about, for they fill him

---

[4]Donald G. Barnhouse, *Revelation: An Expository Commentary* (Grand Rapids: Zondervan, 1971), p. 94. Used by permission.

with delight. But he now witnesses a seventh event,
which causes despair to flood his soul. The crisis
of a seven-sealed book is about to begin!
What is this book (really a rolled-up scroll),
sealed so securely with seven seals? Whatever it
contained, the scroll was extremely important, for
history informs us that under Roman law
all legal documents pertaining to life and death
were to be sealed seven times. A number of
theologians believe that this is actually the legal title
deed to the earth. Thus the angels' proclamation
was, in effect,

"Who is worthy to reclaim the earth's title deed?
Who is able to pour out the seven-sealed judgment,
to purify this planet, and to usher in the long-
awaited golden-age millennium?"

Who indeed *was* worthy?

B. *The Investigation*

"And no man in heaven, nor in earth, neither under
the earth, was able to open the book, neither to
look thereon" (Rev. 5:3).

Let us follow the angel as he begins his threefold search.

1. The search in heaven

Was there any among the redeemed worthy
to claim the earth's title deed? There was not!

> a. Adam originally possessed this title deed
> (Gen. 1:28, 29), but was cheated out of it
> by the Devil (Gen. 3:1-19).

> b. Noah, the hero of the flood, subsequently

became the drunkard of the vineyard,
thus disqualifying himself (Gen. 6—9).

c. Abraham, the father of Israel, backslid and
went to Egypt temporarily (Gen. 12).

d. David, the man after God's own heart,
(1 Sam. 16:7), later broke God's heart
through lust and murder (2 Sam. 11).

e. John the Baptist, the forerunner of Christ,
in a moment of weakness doubted that same
Messiah (Matt. 11:3).

f. Peter, the "rock," denied his Lord
in the hour of need (Matt. 26:70).

g. Paul, perhaps the greatest Christian who
ever lived, compromised his testimony
(Acts 21).

2. The search on earth

Who could accomplish in the sinful environment
of earth what no man could achieve even in the sinless environment of heaven? Preachers and priests
might minister to the earth, and kings rule
over sections of it, but *claim* it they could not!

3. The search under the earth (in hades)

If no saint or angel *could* purify this earth,
then certainly no sinner or demon *would,* even if
this were possible!

C. *The Lamentation*

"And I wept much, because no man was found

worthy to open and to read the book, neither to
look thereon" (Rev. 5:4).

Why did John weep? Perhaps because (among other
things) he realized that the ultimate resurrection
and glorification of his own body was directly connected
with the removal of the curse placed upon this earth!
(See Romans 8:17-23.)

D. The Manifestation

"And one of the elders saith unto me, Weep not:
behold, the Lion of the tribe of Juda, the Root of David,
hath prevailed to open the book, and to loose the seven
seals thereof. And I beheld, and, lo, in the midst
of the throne and of the four beasts, and in the midst
of the elders, stood a Lamb as it had been slain, having
seven horns and seven eyes, which are the seven Spirits
of God sent forth into all the earth. And he came
and took the book out of the right hand of him that
sat upon the throne" (Rev. 5:5-7).

Who is this heavenly Hero who so boldly removes
the scroll from the Father's right hand? We need not
speculate for one second about his identity, for he is
the Lord Jesus Christ himself! The proof is overwhelming.

1. He has the characteristics of a lamb.

Our Lord is referred to as a lamb twenty-nine times
in the New Testament. In all but one instance
(1 Pet. 1:19) it is the Apostle John who
employs this title. Furthermore,

a. It is a pet lamb.

There are two words for "lamb" in the Greek
New Testament. One is *amnos* (a lamb in

general) and the other is *arnion* (a special household pet lamb). Here in Revelation 5:6 the second Greek word is used. For a related Old Testament passage, see 2 Samuel 12:1-4.

b. It is a slain lamb.

Here the Greek word for slain is *sphatto*, and refers to a violent death of some sort. The same word is found in the following passage: ". . . we should love one another. Not as Cain, who was of that wicked one, and slew his brother" (1 John 3:11, 12).

The word *sphatto* is found only seven times in the New Testament, and four of these usages refer to the death of Christ (Rev. 5:6, 9, 12; 13:8).

c. It is an all-powerful lamb.

The lamb is pictured as possessing seven horns, which in biblical symbolic language refers to power and authority.

d. It is an all-knowing lamb.

The lamb is pictured as possessing seven eyes, referring to perfect knowledge and wisdom.

2. He has the characteristics of a lion.

John calls him "The Lion of the tribe of Juda, the Root of David," and so he is. Three key Bible chapters explain this title.

a. In Genesis 49 the dying Jacob predicted that Judah, his fourth son, would be like a lion, and that the later kings of Israel, including

Christ himself, would come from his tribe (Gen. 49:8-10).

b. In 2 Samuel 7 God told David (who was of the tribe of Judah) that his kingdom would be eternal and that his household would rule forever (2 Sam. 7:8-17).

c. In Luke 1 the angel Gabriel explained to Mary (who was of the house of David) that her virgin-born son would inherit all the Old Testament promises as found in Genesis 49 and 2 Samuel 7 (Luke 1:30-33).

Thus John sees Christ as a Lamb, since he once came to redeem his people. This was his past work. John also sees him as a lion, for he shall come again to reign over his people. This will be his future work. The *source* of his claim to the earth's scepter is therefore related to his slain Lamb characteristics while the *strength* of his claim is due to his mighty Lion characteristics!

E. The Adoration

"And they sung a new song, saying, Thou art worthy to take the book, and to open the seals thereof, for thou wast slain, and hast redeemed us to God by thy blood out of every kindred, and tongue, and people, and nation, and hast made us unto our God kings and priests; and we shall reign on the earth.
"And I beheld, and I heard the voice of many angels round about the throne, and the beasts and the elders; and the number of them was ten thousand times ten thousand, and thousands of thousands, saying

with a loud voice, Worthy is the Lamb that was slain
to receive power and riches and wisdom and strength
and honour and glory and blessing.
"And every creature which is in heaven, and on the earth,
and under the earth, and such as are in the sea,
and all that are in them, heard I saying, Blessing
and honour and glory and power be unto him
that sitteth upon the throne, and unto the Lamb for ever
and ever.
"And the four beasts said, Amen. And the four and
twenty elders fell down and worshipped him that liveth
for ever and ever" (Rev. 5:9-14).

V. THE TRIBULATION

A discouraged and despondent Job once exclaimed
in despair, "Man that is born of a woman is of few days,
and full of trouble. He cometh forth like a flower,
and is cut down; he fleeth also as a shadow,
and continueth not" (Job 14:1, 2).

Job's pessimistic description is tragically true for the
unsaved man, apart from the grace of God.
Throughout his tortured and sinful history he has been
subjected to calamities, disasters, and plagues,
which have tracked him as a wolf would a rabbit.
Here is a brief survey of some of the more tragic disasters.

A. Epidemics

1. During 1340-1350 over 25,000,000 people
in Asia and Europe died of the Black Death.
2. In 1545 typhus killed 250,000 in Cuba alone.
3. In 1560 over 3,000,000 died of smallpox
in Brazil.
4. In 1680 diphtheria killed 8000 in Naples, Italy.
5. In 1792 nearly 1,000,000 perished in Egypt
of the Black Plague.
6. In 1802 yellow fever killed 30,000
of Napoleon's soldiers in Santo Domingo.
7. In 1827 Europe lost 900,000 due to cholera.
8. In 1851 tuberculosis killed 51,000 in England.
9. In 1863 30,000 died of scarlet fever in
England.
10. In 1918 some 30,000,000 perished during
the worldwide epidemic of influenza.

B. Volcanic Action

In 1902 Mount Pelee erupted in the West Indies, killing over 30,000 people.

C. Earthquakes

On January 24, 1556 some 830,000 died in China after a massive earthquake.

D. Fires

On December 30, 1903, the most tragic fire in U. S. history killed 600 people who had packed the Iroquois Theater in Chicago, Illinois.

E. Tornadoes

On March 18, 1925, nearly 700 people living in Illinois, Indiana, and Missouri lost their lives in a tornado.

F. Famines

In 1877 nearly 1,000,000 people starved to death in Northern China alone.

G. Floods

In 1887 China lost 900,000 due to one mighty flood.

H. Landslides

On December 16, 1891, 200,000 died in China because of a landslide.

I. Cyclones

On November 12, 1970, over 500,000 fell victim
to a killer waterstorm in East Pakistan.

J. Auto Deaths

Nearly 50,000 were killed by cars in the U. S. alone
during 1965.

The point of all the above gruesome statistics is this:
catastrophe has been man's constant companion
throughout recorded history. But according to the Bible
there is coming a calamity unlike any which this weary
world has ever seen! Although this future period
will be relatively short, it will nevertheless destroy
more of this earth's population than all of the previously
quoted figures combined! In fact, nearly one billion
people will be struck down during the *beginning*
of this terrible coming disaster!

K. The Names for this Period

No less than twelve titles for this blood-chilling period
can be found in the Bible.

    1. The day of the Lord.

This title is used more frequently than any other.
See, for example, Isaiah 2:12; 13:6, 9;
Ezek. 13:5; 30:3; Joel 1:15; 2:1, 11, 31; 3:14;
Amos 5:18, 20; Obadiah 15; Zephaniah 1:7, 14;
Zechariah 14:1; Malachi 4:5; Acts 2:20;
1 Thessalonians 5:2; 2 Thessalonians 2:2;
2 Peter 3:10.

A distinction should be made between the day

of the Lord and the day of Christ. The day
of Christ is a reference to the millennium.
See 1 Corinthians 1:8; 5:5; 2 Corinthians 1:14;
Philippians 1:6, 10; 2:16.

2. The day of God's vengeance (Isa. 34:8;
63:1-6).

3. The time of Jacob's trouble (Jer. 30:7).

4. The seventieth week (Dan. 9:24-27).

5. The time of the end (Dan. 12:9).

6. The great day of his wrath (Rev. 6:17).

7. The hour of his judgment (Rev. 14:7).

8. The end of this world (Matt. 13:40, 49).

9. The indignation (Isa. 26:20; 34:2).

10. The overspreading of abominations
(Dan. 9:27).

11. The time of trouble such as never was
(Dan. 12:1).

12. The tribulation (Matt. 24:21, 29).

The word "tribulation" is derived from the Latin
tribulum, which was an agricultural tool used for
separating the husks from the corn. As found in the Bible,
the theological implications would include such concepts
as a pressing together, an affliction, a burdening
with anguish and trouble, a binding with oppression.

Keeping this in mind, it would seem that of all the

twelve names for the coming calamity the last one would most accurately describe this period. Therefore from this point on, the term *Tribulation* will be employed.

L. *The Nature of the Tribulation*

The following passages aptly describe this future and fearful time.

"Howl ye, for the day of the Lord is at hand. . . . Therefore shall all hands be faint, and every man's heart shall melt. . . . For the stars of heaven and the constellations thereof shall not give their light; the sun shall be darkened in his going forth, and the moon shall not cause her light to shine. . . . And I will punish the world for their evil . . ." (Isa. 13:6, 7, 10, 11).
"And they shall go into the holes of the rocks and into the caves of the earth for fear of the Lord . . . when he ariseth to shake terribly the earth" (Isa. 2:19).
"Behold, the Lord maketh the earth empty . . . and turneth it upside down, and scattereth abroad the inhabitants thereof. . . . The earth is utterly broken down, the earth is clean dissolved, the earth is moved exceedingly. The earth shall reel to and fro like a drunkard . . ." (Isa. 24:1, 19, 20).
"For the indignation of the Lord is upon all nations, and his fury upon all their armies. . . . Their slain also shall be cast out, and their stink shall come up out of their carcasses, and the mountains shall be melted with their blood. And all the host of heaven shall be dissolved, and the heavens shall be rolled together as a scroll . . ." (Isa. 34:2-4).
"I have trodden the winepress alone . . . for I will tread them in mine anger, and trample them in my fury; and their blood shall be sprinkled upon my garments,

and I will stain all my raiment. For the day of vengeance
is in mine heart. . . . And I will tread down the people
in mine anger, and make them drunk in my fury . . ."
(Isa. 63:3, 4, 6).
"Thus saith the Lord of hosts, Behold, evil shall
go forth from nation to nation, and a great whirlwind
shall be raised up from the coasts of the earth.
And the slain of the Lord shall be at that day from one
end of the earth even unto the other end of the earth;
they shall not be lamented, neither gathered,
nor buried . . ." (Jer. 25:32, 33).
"Blow ye the trumpet in Zion, and sound an alarm
in my holy mountain: let all the inhabitants of the land
tremble, for the day of the Lord cometh . . . a day
of darkness and of gloominess, a day of clouds . . . there
hath not been ever the like, neither shall be any more
after it . . ." (Joel 2:1, 2).
"The great day of the Lord is near . . . that day is a day
of wrath, a day of trouble and distress . . ."
(Zeph. 1:14, 15).
"For nation shall rise against nation, and kingdom
against kingdom; and there shall be famines and pestilences
and earthquakes in divers places. . . . And many
false prophets shall rise, and shall deceive many.
And because iniquity shall abound, the love of many
shall wax cold. . . . For then shall be great tribulation,
such as was not since the beginning of the world to this
time, no, nor ever shall be. And except those days
should be shortened, there should no flesh be saved . . ."
(Matt. 24:7, 11, 12, 21, 22).
"And there shall be signs in the sun and in the moon
and in the stars, and upon the earth distress of nations,
with perplexity, the sea and the waves roaring,
men's hearts failing them for fear . . . for the powers
of heaven shall be shaken" (Luke 21:25, 26).

". . . the day of the Lord so cometh as a thief in the night.
For when they shall say, Peace and safety, then sudden
destruction cometh upon them, as travail upon a woman
with child; and they shall not escape" (1 Thess. 5:2, 3).
". . . and, lo, there was a great earthquake; and the sun
became black as sackcloth of hair, and the moon
became as blood; and the stars of heaven fell
unto the earth, even as a fig tree casteth her untimely figs,
when she is shaken of a mighty wind. And the heaven
departed as a scroll when it is rolled together;
and every mountain and island were moved out of
their places. And the kings of the earth, and the great men,
and the rich men, and the chief captains, and the
mighty men, and every bondman, and every free man,
hid themselves in the dens and in the rocks of the
mountains, and said to the mountains and rocks,
Fall on us, and hide us from the face of him that sitteth
on the throne, and from the wrath of the Lamb,
for the great day of his wrath is come; and who shall
be able to stand?" (Rev. 6:12-17).

M. The Length of the Tribulation

To establish this time-span we must now briefly
consider the most important, the most amazing,
and the most profound single prophecy in the entire
Word of God! It is often referred to as the prophecy
of the Seventy Weeks, and was written by Daniel,
who was living in Babylon around 550 B.C. Daniel,
a former Jewish captive, had been reading Jeremiah's
prophecy, which predicted that after a seventy-year
captivity period, God would permit the Jews to return
to Jerusalem (Jer. 25:11; 29:10). As Daniel studied
those words he began to pray, confessing both his sins
and the sins of Israel. During this powerful and

tearful prayer, the angel Gabriel appeared to Daniel
and related to him the prophecy of the Seventy Weeks,
which reads as follows:

"Seventy weeks are determined upon thy people and upon
thy holy city, to finish the transgression, and to make
an end of sins, and to make reconciliation for iniquity,
and to bring in everlasting righteousness, and to seal up
the vision and prophecy, and to anoint the most holy.

"Know therefore and understand, that from the going forth
of the commandment to restore and to build Jerusalem
unto the Messiah the Prince shall be seven weeks,
and threescore and two weeks; the street shall be built
again, and the wall, even in troublous times.

"And after threescore and two weeks shall Messiah
be cut off, but not for himself; and the people of the prince
that shall come shall destroy the city and the sanctuary;
and the end thereof shall be with a flood,
and unto the end of the war desolations are determined.

"And he shall confirm the covenant with many
for one week: and in the midst of the week he shall
cause the sacrifice and the oblation to cease,
and for the overspreading of abominations he shall
make it desolate, even until the consummation,
and that determined shall be poured upon the desolate"
(Dan. 9:24-27).

1. To whom does this prophecy refer? It refers
to Israel!

2. What is meant by the term "seventy weeks"?

In his correspondence course on the book of Daniel,
Dr. Alfred Martin of Moody Bible Institute
writes the following helpful words:

"The expression translated 'seventy weeks'

is literally 'seventy sevens.' Apart from the context
one would not know what the 'sevens' were.
One would have to inquire, 'seven of what?'
This expression in Hebrew would be as ambiguous
as if one were to say in English, 'I went to the store
and bought a dozen.' A dozen of what?

"One of the basic principles of interpretation is
that one must always interpret in the light of the
context, that is, in the light of the passage
in which a given statement occurs. As one searches
this context, remembering that the vision was given
in answer to the prayer, one notes that Daniel
had been reading in Jeremiah that God would
'accomplish seventy years in the desolations
of Jerusalem' (Dan. 9:2). This is the clue.
Daniel is told in effect, 'Yes, God will accomplish
seventy years in the captivity; but now He
is showing you that the whole history of the people
of Israel will be consummated in a period
of seventy sevens of years.' "[5]

To further clarify the meaning of the Seventy Weeks,
it should be noted that Israel had in its
calendar not only a week of seven days
(as in Exod. 23:12), but also a "week" of seven
years (Lev. 25:3, 4, 8-10; Gen. 29:27, 28).
In other words, God is here telling Daniel
that he would continue to deal with Israel
for another 490 years before bringing in everlasting
righteousness!

3. When was the seventy-week period to begin?

It was to begin with the command to rebuild

---

[5]Alfred Martin, *Daniel, the Framework of Prophecy* (Chicago: Moody Correspondence School, 820 N. LaSalle St. 1963), pp. 85, 86. Used by permission.

Jerusalem's walls. The first two chapters
of Nehemiah inform us that this command was
issued during the twentieth year of Artaxerxes'
accession. The *Encyclopaedia Britannica* sets
this date on March 14, 445 B.C.

4. What are the four distinct time periods
mentioned within the seventy-week prophecy
and what was to happen during each period?

a. First period

Seven weeks (forty-nine years), from 445 B.C.
to 396 B.C. The key event during this time
was the building of the streets and walls
of Jerusalem "even in troublous times."
This literally took place! See Nehemiah 2—6.

b. Second period

Sixty-two weeks (434 years), from 396 B.C.
to A.D. 30. At the end of this second period
the Messiah was crucified! See Matthew 27,
Mark 15, Luke 23, and John 19.

The brilliant British scholar and Bible student,
Sir Robert Anderson, has reduced the first two
periods into their exact number of days. This he has
done by multiplying 483 (the combined years
of the first two periods) by 360 (the days in a
biblical year, as pointed out in Genesis 7:11, 24;
8:3, 4).

The total number of days in the first sixty-nine
weeks (or 483 years) is 173,880. Anderson
then points out that if one begins counting on
March 14, 445 B.C., and goes forward in history,
these days would run out on April 6, A.D. 32.

*It was on this very day that Jesus made his
triumphal entry into the city of Jerusalem!*
Surely our Lord must have had Daniel's prophecy
in mind when he said, "If thou hadst known,
even thou, at least in this thy day, the things
which belong to thy peace! But now they are hid
from thine eyes" (Luke 19:42).

Of course, it was also on this same day that the
Pharisees plotted to murder Christ (Luke 19:47).
Thus Daniel, writing some five-and-one-half
centuries earlier, correctly predicted the very day
of Christ's presentation and rejection!

> c. Third period
> One-half week (3½ years), the first half
> of the Tribulation. At the beginning of
> this period the antichrist will make a seven-year
> pact with Israel.

> d. Fourth period
> One-half week (3½ years), the last half
> of the Tribulation. At the beginning of this
> period the antichrist will break his pact
> with Israel and will begin his terrible
> bloodbath. At the end of the last week
> (and of the entire seventy-week period),
> the true Messiah will come and establish
> his perfect millennium!

5. Do the Seventy Weeks run continuously?
That is to say, is there a gap somewhere between
these 490 years, or do they run without pause
until they are completed?

Dispensational theology teaches that these "weeks"
do not run continuously, but that there has been

a gap or parenthesis of nearly 2000 years
between the sixty-ninth and seventieth week.

The chronology may be likened to a seventy-minute
basketball game. For sixty-nine minutes the game
has been played at a furious and continuous pace.
Then the referee for some reason calls time out
with the clock in the red and showing one final
minute of play. No one knows for sure when
the action will start again, but at some point
the referee will step in and blow his whistle.
At that time the teams will gather to play out
the last minute of the game.

God has stepped in and stopped the clock
of prophecy at Calvary. This divine "time out"
has already lasted some twenty centuries,
but soon now the Redeemer will blow his trumpet
and the final "week" of action will be played
upon this earth!

6.   Does the Bible offer any other examples
of time gaps in divine programs? It does indeed.
At least three instances come to mind in which gaps
of many centuries can be found in a single short
paragraph.

    a.   Isaiah 9:6, 7

    "For unto us a child is born, unto us a
    son is given: and the government shall be
    upon his shoulder; and his name shall be called
    Wonderful, Counselor, The mighty God,
    The everlasting Father, The Prince of Peace.
    Of the increase of his government and peace
    there shall be no end, upon the throne
    of David, and upon his kingdom. . . ."

In the first part of verse 6 a gap of at least twenty centuries is separated by a colon. The phrase "unto us a son is given" refers to Bethlehem, while the words "and the government shall be upon his shoulder" look forward to the millennium.

b. Zechariah 9:9, 10

"Rejoice greatly, O daughter of Zion; shout, O daughter of Jerusalem; behold, thy King cometh unto thee: he is just, and having salvation; lowly, and riding upon an ass, and upon a colt the foal of an ass. . . . And he shall speak peace unto the heathen, and his dominion shall be from sea even to sea, and from the river even to the ends of the earth."

Verse 9 is a clear reference to the triumphal entry of our Lord, but verse 10 looks ahead to the millennium.

c. Isaiah 61:1, 2

"The Spirit of the Lord God is upon me, because the Lord hath anointed me to preach good tidings unto the meek; he hath sent me to bind up the brokenhearted, to proclaim liberty to the captives, and the opening of the prison to them that are bound; to proclaim the acceptable year of the Lord, and the day of vengeance of our God. . . ."

In verse 2 of this passage Christ's earthly ministry (to "proclaim the acceptable year of the Lord") and the Tribulation (the "day of vengeance of our God") are separated by only a comma! It is extremely

important to note that when Jesus read this
passage during his sermon in Nazareth,
he ended the reading at this comma, for
"the day of vengeance" was not the purpose
of his first coming! See Luke 4:18, 19.

N. *The Purpose of the Tribulation*

Why this terrible period? At least six scriptural reasons
are forthcoming:

1. To harvest the crop that has been sown
throughout the ages by God, Satan, and mankind.
This aspect is so important that our Lord took
an entire sermon to discuss it. Portions of his
message are as follows:

a. The first part of the sermon proclaimed:

"Behold, a sower went forth to sow. And
when he sowed, some seeds fell by the wayside,
and the fowls came and devoured them up;
some fell upon stony places, where they
had not much earth; and forthwith they
sprung up, because they had no deepness
of earth; and when the sun was up, they
were scorched; and because they had no root,
they withered away. And some fell
among thorns; and the thorns sprung up,
and choked them; but other fell into
good ground, and brought forth fruit,
some an hundredfold, some sixtyfold,
some thirtyfold" (Matt. 13:3-8).

b. The first part of the sermon explained:

"Hear ye therefore the parable of the sower.

When anyone heareth the word of the
kingdom, and understandeth it not,
then cometh the wicked one, and catcheth
away that which was sown in his heart.
This is he which received seed by the wayside.
But he that received the seed into stony
places, the same is he that heareth the word,
and at once with joy receiveth it,
yet hath not root in himself, but dureth
for a while; for when tribulation or persecution
ariseth because of the word, by and by
he is offended.

"He also that received seed among the thorns
is he that heareth the word; and the care
of this world and the deceitfulness of riches
choke the word, and he becometh unfruitful.

"But he that received seed into the good
ground is he that heareth the word
and understandeth it, which also beareth fruit
and bringeth forth, some an hundredfold,
some sixty, some thirty" (Matt. 13:18-23).

c. The second part of the sermon proclaimed:

"The kingdom of heaven is likened
unto a man which sowed good seed in his field;
but while men slept, his enemy came
and sowed tares among the wheat, and
went his way. But when the blade was
sprung up and brought forth fruit, then
appeared the tares also. So the servants
of the householder came and said unto him,
Sir, didst not thou sow good seed
in the field? From whence then hath it tares?
He said unto them, An enemy hath done this.
The servants said unto him, Wilt thou

then that we go and gather them up?
But he said, Nay, lest while ye gather up
the tares, ye root up also the wheat with them.
Let both grow together until the harvest;
and in the time of harvest I will say to the
reapers, gather ye together first the tares,
and bind them in bundles to burn them;
but gather the wheat into my barn"
(Matt. 13:24-30).

d. The second part of the sermon explained:

"He that soweth the good seed is the Son
of man; the field is the world; the good seed
are the children of the kingdom; but the tares
are the children of the wicked one;
the enemy that sowed them is the devil;
the harvest is the end of the world; and the
reapers are the angels. As therefore the tares
are gathered and burned in the fire,
so shall it be in the end of this world.
The Son of man shall send forth his angels,
and they shall gather out of his kingdom
all things that offend, and them which do
iniquity; and shall cast them into a furnace
of fire: there shall be wailing and
gnashing of teeth. Then shall the righteous
shine forth as the sun in the kingdom
of their Father" (Matt. 13:37-43).

2. To prove the falseness of the Devil's claim.

Since his fall (Isa. 14:12-14), Satan has been
attempting to convince a skeptical universe that
he rather than Christ is the logical and rightful ruler
of creation. Therefore, during the Tribulation
the sovereign God will give him a free and

unhindered hand to make good his boast. Needless to say, Satan will fail miserably!

3. To prepare a great martyred multitude for heaven.

"After this I beheld, and, lo, a great multitude, which no man could number, of all nations and kindreds and people and tongues, stood before the throne. . . . These are they which came out of great tribulation, and have washed their robes, and made them white in the blood of the lamb" (Rev. 7:9, 14).

4. To prepare a great living multitude for the millennium.

"And before him shall be gathered all nations; and he shall separate them one from another, as a shepherd divideth his sheep from the goats; and he shall set the sheep on his right hand, but the goats on the left. Then shall the king say unto them on his right hand, Come, ye blessed of my Father, inherit the kingdom prepared for you from the foundation of the world" (Matt. 25:32-34).

5. To punish the Gentiles.

"For the wrath of God is revealed from heaven against all ungodliness and unrighteousness of men . . ." (Rom. 1:18).
"And for this cause God shall send them strong delusion, that they should believe a lie, that they all might be damned who believe not the truth, but had pleasure in unrighteousness" (2 Thess. 2:11, 12).
"And out of his mouth goeth a sharp sword,

that with it he should smite the nations"
(Rev. 19:15).

6. To purge Israel.

"And I will cause you to pass under the rod . . . and
I will purge out from among you the rebels . . ."
(Ezek. 20:37, 38).
"And it shall come to pass, that in all the land,
saith the Lord, two parts therein shall be cut off
and die; but the third shall be left therein.
And I will bring the third part through the fire,
and will refine them as silver is refined, and
will try them as gold is tried; they shall call
on my name, and I will hear them: I will say,
it is my people; and they shall say, The Lord
is my God" (Zech. 13:8, 9).
"And he shall sit as a refiner and purifier of silver;
and he shall purify the sons of Levi, and purge them
as gold and silver, that they may offer unto the Lord
an offering in righteousness" (Mal. 3:3).

O. The Personalities of the Tribulation

As in an ancient Shakespearean play, a number
of actors will render their parts and say their lines
during the earth's most sobering drama, the Tribulation!

1. The Holy Spirit

Contrary to some, the Holy Spirit will *not*
be removed when the church is raptured! He will
instead (it would seem) perform a ministry
similar to his work in the Old Testament.
At any rate, his presence will be felt in the Tribulation, as indicated by the Prophet Joel.

"And it shall come to pass afterward, that I will
pour out my Spirit upon all flesh. . . . And I will
shew wonders in the heavens and in the earth,
blood and fire, and pillars of smoke. The sun
shall be turned into darkness, and the moon
into blood, before the great and the terrible day
of the Lord come. And it shall come to pass,
that whosoever shall call on the name of the Lord
shall be delivered" (Joel 2:28, 30-32).

2. The Devil

"Woe to the inhabiters of the earth and of the sea!
For the devil is come down unto you, having
great wrath, because he knoweth that he hath
but a short time" (Rev. 12:12).

3. Two special Old Testament (?) witnesses

"And I will give power unto my two witnesses,
and they shall prophesy a thousand two hundred
and threescore days, clothed in sackcloth"
(Rev. 11:3).

Who are these witnesses?

> a. Some hold that they are Elijah and Enoch.
> Hebrews 9:27 states that all men are
> appointed to die, and since these two men
> did not experience physical death, they will be
> sent back to witness and to eventually die
> a martyr's death.

> b. Some hold that they are Elijah and Moses.
>
> *Elijah*
>
> (1) Because of Malachi 4:5, 6,
> which predicts that God will send Elijah

during that great and dreadful day
of the Lord.
(2) Because Elijah appeared with
Moses on the Mount of Transfiguration
to talk with Jesus (Matt. 17:3).
(3) Because Elijah's Old Testament
ministry of preventing rain for some three
years will be repeated by one of the
witnesses during the Tribulation.
(Compare 1 Kings 17:1 with Revelation
11:6.)

Moses

(1) Because of Jude 9, where we are
informed that after the death of Moses
Satan attempted to acquire his dead body,
so that God would not be able to use him
against the antichrist during the
Tribulation.
(2) Because Moses' Old Testament
ministry of turning water into blood
will be repeated by one of the witnesses
during the Tribulation. (Compare
Exodus 7:19 with Revelation 11:6.)
(3) Because Moses appeared with
Elijah on the Mount of Transfiguration
(Matt. 17:3).

4. The Antichrist

"And he shall speak great words against
the most High, and shall wear out the saints
of the most High . . ." (Dan. 7:25).
"And the king shall do according to his will;
and he shall exalt himself, and magnify himself

above every god, and shall speak . . . things against
the God of gods . . ." (Dan. 11:36).
". . . that man of sin . . . the son of perdition,
who opposeth and exalteth himself above all
that is called God or that is worshiped,
so that he as God sitteth in the temple of God,
shewing himself that he is God. . . . Even him whose
coming is after the working of Satan, with all power
and signs and lying wonders" (2 Thess. 2:3, 4, 9).
"Who is a liar but he that denieth that Jesus is
the Christ? He is antichrist that denieth
the Father and the Son" (1 John 2:22).
"And I saw, and behold a white horse;
and he that sat on him had a bow, and a crown
was given unto him; and he went forth conquering
and to conquer" (Rev. 6:2).
"And I stood upon the sand of the sea and saw a
beast rise up out of the sea. . . . And the beast
which I saw was like unto a leopard, and his feet
were as the feet of a bear, and his mouth as the
mouth of a lion; and the dragon gave him his power
. . . and great authority. . . . And he opened
his mouth in blasphemy against God . . ."
(Rev. 13:1, 2, 6).

These passages describe for us the most powerful
and perverted person who will ever walk the paths
of this earth. We shall briefly examine this vile
and vicious man along the following lines:

    a. His personal characteristics

        (1) He will be an intellectual genius
        (Dan. 8:23).
        (2) He will be an oratorical genius
        (Dan. 11:36).

(3)   He will be a political genius
(Rev. 17:11, 12).
(4)   He will be a commercial genius
(Rev. 13:16, 17; Dan. 11:43).
(5)   He will be a military genius
(Rev. 6:2; 13:4).
(6)   He will be a religious genius
(Rev. 13:8; 2 Thess. 2:4).

b.   His various names and titles (in addition to
that of the antichrist)

(1)   The man of sin (2 Thess. 2:3)
(2)   The son of perdition (2 Thess. 2:3)
(3)   The wicked one (2 Thess. 2:8)
(4)   The willful king (Dan. 11:36)
(5)   The beast (Rev. 11:7. This title is
found thirty-six times in the book
of Revelation.)
(6)   The little horn (Dan. 7:8)

c.   His Old Testament forerunners

Just as there are many Old Testament
characters which depict the person and work
of the Lord Jesus (such as Melchizedek
in Genesis 14 and Isaac in Genesis 22),
there are a number of Old Testament men
who describe for us the coming ministry
of the antichrist.

(1)   Cain — by his murder of the chosen
seed (Gen. 4:5-14; Jude 11; 1 John
3:12)
(2)   Nimrod — by his creation of
Babylon and the tower of Babel
(Gen. 10, 11)
(3)   Pharaoh — by his oppression

of God's people (Exod. 1:8-22)
(4) Korah — by his rebellion (Num. 16:1-3; Jude 11)
(5) Balaam — by his attempt to curse Israel (Num. 23, 24; 2 Peter 2:15; Jude 11; Rev. 2:14)
(6) Saul — by his intrusion into the office of the priesthood (1 Sam. 13:9-13)
(7) Goliath — by his proud boasting (1 Sam. 17)
(8) Absalom — by his attempt to steal the throne of David (2 Sam. 15:1-6)
(9) Jeroboam — by his substitute religion (1 Kings 12:25-31)
(10) Sennacherib — by his efforts to destroy Jerusalem (2 Kings 18:17)
(11) Nebuchadnezzar — by his golden statue (Dan. 3:1-7)
(12) Haman — by his plot to exterminate the Jews (Esther 3)
(13) Antiochus Epiphanes — by his defilement of the temple (Dan. 11:21-35)

d. His identity

(1) Some believe the antichrist will be a Gentile, since he comes from the sea (Rev. 13:1), which is often a symbol for Gentile and heathen nations.

(2) Some believe he will be a resurrected individual, on the basis of Revelation 13:3 and 17:8.

(3) Some believe he will be Judas Iscariot, on the basis of the following verses:

John 6:70, 71. Here Jesus refers to Judas as the Devil.

Luke 22:3; John 13:27. Here Satan actually enters Judas. This is never said of any other individual in the Bible.

John 17:12; 2 Thess. 2:3. The title "son of perdition" is only found twice in the New Testament. In the first instance Jesus used it to refer to Judas. In the second instance Paul used it to refer to the antichrist.

Acts 1:25. Here Peter says that Judas after his death went "to his own place." Some have seen in this a reference to the bottomless pit, and believe that Satan has retained Judas here for the past 2000 years in preparation for his future role of the antichrist!

e.   His rise to power

(1)   Through the power of Satan (Rev. 13:4; 2 Thess. 2:3, 9-12).

(2)   Through the permission of the Holy Spirit. His present-day manifestation is being hindered by the Holy Spirit until the Rapture of the church. God is in control of all situations down here and will continue to be! (See Job 1 and 2, 2 Thessalonians 2:6, 7).

(3)   Through the formation of a ten-nation organization.

He will proceed from a ten-dictatorship confederation which will come into

existence during the Tribulation.
These dictators are referred to as ten
horns in Daniel 7:7; Revelation 12:3;
13:1; 17:7, 12. In his rise to power
he will defeat three of these dictators
(Dan. 7:8, 24). This ten-horned
confederation is the Revived Roman
Empire. This is derived from the fact
that the most important prophetic details
concerning the Old Roman Empire
in Daniel 2:40-44 are still unfulfilled.

The Revived Roman Empire is the last
of seven Gentile world powers to plague
the nation Israel. These powers are
referred to as seven heads in Revelation
12:3; 13:1; 17:7. They are:
Egypt, which enslaved Israel for
400 years (Exod. 1—12).
Assyria, which captured the Northern
Kingdom of Israel (2 Kings 17).
Babylon, which captured the Southern
Kingdom of Israel (2 Kings 24).
Persia, which produced wicked Haman
(Esth. 3).
Greece, which produced, indirectly,
Antiochus Epiphanes (Dan. 11).
Rome, which destroyed Jerusalem in
A.D. 70 (see Luke 21) and which will
hound Israel in the Revived Empire
as never before in all history (Rev. 12).

(4) Through the cooperation of the
false religious system (Rev. 17).

(5) Through his personal charisma
and ability.

(6) Through a false (or real?) resurrection (Rev. 13:3).

(7) Through a false peace program, probably in the Middle East (Dan. 8:25).

(8) Through a master plan of deception and trickery (Matt. 24:24; 2 Thess. 2:9; Rev. 13:14).

f. His activities

(1) He begins by controlling the western power block (Rev. 17:12).
(2) He makes a seven-year covenant with Israel but breaks it after 3½ years (Dan. 9:27).
(3) He gains absolute control over the Middle East after the Russian invasion (Ezek. 38, 39).
(4) He attempts to destroy all of Israel (Rev. 12).
(5) He destroys the false religious system, so that he may rule unhindered (Rev. 17:16, 17).
(6) He thereupon sets himself up as God (Dan. 11:36, 37; 2 Thess. 2:4 11; Rev. 13:5).
(7) He briefly rules over all nations (Psa. 2; Dan. 11:36; Rev. 13:16).
(8) He is utterly crushed by the Lord Jesus Christ at the Battle of Armageddon (Rev. 19).
(9) He is the first creature to be thrown into the lake of fire (Rev. 19:20).

The July, 1965, *Reader's Digest* book section condenses the book *A Gift of Prophecy,* written by that famous (but equally false) prophetess Jeane Dixon.

The article concludes with the following words:

"A child born in the Middle East on February 5, 1962 will revolutionize the world and eventually unite all warring creeds and sects into one all-embracing faith. This person, who has been the subject of some of Jeane Dixon's strongest, clearest visions, was born of humble peasant origin. Mankind, she says, will begin to feel the great force of this man about 1980, and his power will grow mightily until 1999, at which time there will be peace on earth to all men of good will."

As we read this we are reminded of the Savior's words to a group of wicked and unbelieving Pharisees: "I am come in my Father's name, and ye receive me not; if another shall come in his own name, him ye will receive" (John 5:43).

g. His amazing ability to imitate.

The antichrist would surely have been a tremendously successful mimic on any late-night TV talk show! Note the following areas in which he will attempt to imitate the person and work of Christ.

> (1) The antichrist comes in the very image of Satan, as Christ came in the image of God. (Compare Rev. 13:4 and 2 Thess. 2:9 with Col. 1:15 and Heb. 1:3.)
> (2) The antichrist is the second person

in the hellish trinity, as Christ is
in the heavenly trinity. (Compare
Rev. 16:13 with Matt. 28:19.)
(3) The antichrist comes up from
the abyss while Christ comes down
from heaven. (Compare Rev. 11:7
and 17:8 with John 6:38.)
(4) The antichrist is a savage beast
while Christ is a sacrificial lamb.
(Compare Rev. 13:2 with Rev. 5:6-9.)
(5) The antichrist receives his power
from Satan, as Christ received his power
from his Father. (Compare Rev. 13:2
with Matt. 28:18.)
(6) The antichrist will experience a
resurrection (perhaps a fake one),
just as Christ experienced a true one!
(Compare Rev. 13:3, 12 with Rom. 1:4.)
(7) The antichrist will receive
the worship of all unbelievers,
as Christ did of all believers. (Compare
Rev. 13:3, 4, 8 and John 5:43
with Matt. 2:11; Luke 24:52; John
20:28; Phil. 2:10, 11.)
(8) The antichrist will deliver mighty
speeches, as did Christ. (Compare
Dan. 7:8 and Rev. 13:5 with John 7:46.)
(9) The greater part of the antichrist's
ministry will last some 3½ years,
about the time span of Christ's ministry.
(Compare Rev. 13:5 and 12:6, 14
with John 2:13; 6:4; 11:55.)
(10) The antichrist will attempt
(unsuccessfully) to combine the three
Old Testament offices of prophet,

priest, and king, as someday Christ will successfully do!

(11) The antichrist's symbolic number is 6, while the symbolic number of Christ is 7. (Compare Rev. 13:18 with Rev. 5:6, 12.)

(12) The antichrist will someday kill his harlot wife, while Christ will someday glorify his holy bride. (Compare Rev. 17:16, 17 with Rev. 21:1, 2.)

5. The False Prophet

"And I beheld another beast coming up out of the earth . . ." (Rev. 13:11).

a. His identity

Who is this second beast of Revelation 13 who is also called on three later occasions "the false prophet" (Rev. 16:13; 19:20; 20:10)? Some believe he will be a Jew (while the antichrist will be a Gentile), and that he will head up the apostate church.

b. His activities

It has already been pointed out that the antichrist will attempt to mimic Christ; it would appear that the false prophet will try to copy the work of the Holy Spirit. Thus the following analogy has been suggested between the Spirit of God and the second beast.

(1) The Holy Spirit is the third person of the heavenly trinity (Matt. 28:19), while the false prophet is the third person of the hellish trinity (Rev. 16:13).

(2) The Holy Spirit leads men into all truth (John 16:13), while the false prophet seduces men into all error (Rev. 13:11, 14).

(3) The Holy Spirit glorifies Christ (John 16:13, 14), while the false prophet glorifies the antichrist (Rev. 13:12).

(4) The Holy Spirit made fire to come down from heaven at Pentecost (Acts 2:3), while the false prophet will do likewise on earth in view of men (Rev. 13:13).

(5) The Holy Spirit gives life (Rom. 8:2), while the false prophet kills (Rev. 13:15).

(6) The Holy Spirit marks with a seal all those who belong to God (Eph. 1:13), while the false prophet marks those who worship Satan (Rev. 13:16, 17).

c. His mark

"And he causeth all, both small and great, rich and poor, free and bond, to receive a mark in their right hand, or in their foreheads; and that no man might buy or sell, save he that had the mark, or the name of the beast, or the number of his name. Here is wisdom. Let him that hath understanding count the number of the beast, for it is the number of a man; and his number is six hundred threescore and six" (Rev. 13:16-18).

Perhaps no other single passage in the

Word of God has been the object of more silly
and serious speculation than this one.
How are we to understand the number 666?
In concluding this section, we shall quote
from two well-known authors:

"In Greek (as in Hebrew and in Latin)
the letters of the alphabet serve likewise
as signs for the figures. Alpha signifies one;
beta, two, etc. For any name it is, therefore,
possible to add together the numerical value
of each letter and to arrive at a total
which forms 'the number of a man.'
The name of the antichrist will give the total
of 666. Men have sought to apply this method
with reference to all the persons in history
who have seemed to be the antichrist.
By more or less arranging the letters of the titles
of these persons they have arrived at the
number 666 for the names of Nero,
Mohammed, the Pope, Napoleon, and even
Hitler, not to speak of many others. In our
opinion the proof that these interpretations
are still premature is that they are all
contradictory. We are convinced that when
the last and great antichrist appears,
the true believers of the entire world will
recognize him. The Holy Spirit will give
to them enough light to calculate unaminously
the number of his name."[6]

"Probably the simplest explanation here
is the best, that the triple six is the number
of a man, each digit falling short of the perfect

---

[6]René Pache. *The Return of Jesus Christ* (Chicago: Moody, 1955), pp. 183,
184. Used by permission.

number seven. Six in the scripture
is man's number. He was to work six days
and rest the seventh. The image
of Nebuchadnezzar was sixty cubits high
and six cubits broad. Whatever may be
the deeper meaning of the number,
it implies that this title, referring to the
first beast, Satan's masterpiece, limits him
to man's level, which is far short of the deity
of Jesus Christ."[7]

Whatever is involved in this hellish mark,
it is apparently very important, for it is
referred to again no less than six times!
(See Rev. 14:9, 11; 15:2; 16:2; 19:20;
20:4.)

6. A multitude of specialized angels

Angels have been employed throughout the Bible
to perform God's work, but at no other time
will they be as busy as during the Tribulation!
The book of Revelation describes the following
for us:

a. Seven angels with seven trumpets
(Rev. 8, 9, 11)
b. Seven angels with seven vials of wrath
(Rev. 16)
c. An angel with the seal of the living God
(Rev. 7:2)
d. An angel with a golden censer (Rev. 8:3)
e. An angel with a little book and
a measuring reed (Rev. 10:1, 2; 11:1)

---

[7]John Walvoord, *The Revelation of Jesus Christ* (Chicago: Moody, 1966),
p. 210. Used by permission.

f. An angel with the everlasting gospel
(Rev. 14:6)
g. An angel with a harvest sickle
(Rev. 14:19)
h. An angel with a message of doom
(Rev. 18:1, 21)
i. An angel with a strange invitation
(Rev. 19:17)
j. An angel with a key and a great chain
(Rev. 20:1)

In the Old Testament the prophet Daniel (Dan.
12:1) informs us that one of these angels will be
Michael the Archangel himself!

7. One-hundred-forty-four thousand Israelite
preachers

No ink will be wasted here refuting the silly
and unscriptural claim of that sect known
as the Jehovah's Witnesses, who brazenly claim
that their devilish group today comprises this
144,000! The Bible clearly teaches that the 144,000
will consist of 12,000 saved and commissioned
preachers from each of the twelve tribes
of Israel (Rev. 7)! It is interesting to compare
the various listings of Israel's twelve tribes
in the Bible. For example, here in Revelation 7
the two tribes of Dan and Ephraim are omitted
and are replaced by Joseph (Ephraim's father)
and Levi (Dan's priestly brother).

We are not told the reason for this omission.
Some believe that Dan is left out because of the hint
(Gen. 49:17; Jer. 8:16) that the antichrist
will come from this tribe. Ephraim's absence

may possibly be accounted for due to their sad tendency to apostatize (Hosea 6:4, 10).

Whatever the reason for their omission here, the glorious fact remains that both Dan and Ephraim take their rightful place in the land of Israel during the millennium! Both are mentioned by Ezekiel (Ezek. 48:2, 5) as he describes the location of the twelve tribes during Christ's thousand-year reign.

Dr. J. Dwight Pentecost offers the following interesting words concerning the conversion of the 144,000:

"In 1 Corinthians 15:8 is a clue concerning the way God will work after the church's rapture. After the apostle had listed those to whom the resurrected Christ appeared, so as to authenticate His resurrection, he says, 'And last of all he was seen of me also, as of one born out of due time.' This phrase, 'born out of due time,' means a premature birth. That is exactly what the apostle Paul is saying — 'I was one that was born prematurely.' What did he mean? Comparing Revelation 7 with Paul's statement in 1 Corinthians 15, we conclude that after the rapture of the church, God will perform the same miracle He performed in Saul of Tarsus on the Damascus Road 144,000 times over."[8]

8. An army of locust-like demons from the bottomless pit (Rev. 9:1-12)

a. The description of these demons
"The locusts looked like horses armored

---

[8]J. Dwight Pentecost, *Will Man Survive?* (Chicago: Moody, 1971), p. 148. Used by permission.

for battle. They had what looked like
golden crowns on their heads, and their faces
looked like men's. Their hair was long
like women's, and their teeth were those
of lions. They wore breastplates that
seemed to be of iron, and their wings roared
like an army of chariots rushing into battle.
They had stinging tails like scorpions,
and their power to hurt, given to them
for five months, was in their tails"
(Rev. 9:7-10, TLB).

b. The destruction by these demons

"They were told not to hurt the grass
or plants or trees, but to attack those people
who did not have the mark of God on their
foreheads. They were not to kill them,
but to torture them for five months
with agony like the pain of scorpion stings.
In those days men will try to kill themselves, but won't be able to — death will
not come. They will long to die — but death
will flee away!" (Rev. 9:4-6, TLB).

In this chapter we learn for the first time
of a place called the bottomless pit.
God mentions it no less than seven times
in the book of Revelation! See Revelation
9:1, 2, 11; 11:7; 17:8; 20:1, 3. It is possible
that this is the same place referred to by both
Peter and Jude in their writings. See 2 Peter
2:4; Jude 6.

9. An army of horse-and-rider demons from
the Euphrates River (Rev. 9:13-21)

a.   Their appearance and actions

"I saw their horses spread out before me
in my vision; their riders wore fiery-red
breastplates, though some were sky-blue
and others yellow. The horses' heads
looked much like lions', and smoke and fire
and flaming sulphur billowed from their
mouths, killing one-third of all mankind.
Their power of death was not only in
their mouths, but in their tails as well,
for their tails were similar to serpents' heads
that struck and bit with fatal wounds"
(Rev. 9:17-19, TLB).

b. Their number

This hellish demonic army will number
200 million strong (Rev. 9:16)!

c. Their leaders

" 'Release the four mighty demons held
bound at the great River Euphrates.' They had
been kept in readiness for that year
and month and day and hour, and now
they were turned loose to kill a third
of all mankind" (Rev. 9:14, 15, TLB).

Thus this fantastic army of 200 million
is led into battle by these four demons!

10.   Three evil spirits

"And I saw three evil spirits disguised as frogs
leap from the mouth of the Dragon, the Creature,
and his False Prophet. These miracle-working
demons conferred with all the rulers of the world
to gather them for battle against the Lord

on that great coming Judgment Day of God
Almighty" (Rev. 16:13, 14, TLB).

11.   A cruel, power-mad ruler from the North

Some 2600 years ago a Hebrew prophet
named Ezekiel prophesied that a wicked and
God-hating nation north of Palestine would rise up
and invade Israel just prior to the second coming
of Christ. He predicts this in Ezekiel 38 and 39,
where we learn the following information:

> a.   That the name of this nation will be Rosh
> (Ezek. 38:2, NASB). In this same verse
> Ezekiel specifies two cities of Rosh,
> Meshech and Tubal. These names are
> remarkably similar to those of Moscow
> and Tobalek, the two ruling city capitals
> of Russia today!

> b.   That the name of the leader of this nation
> will be Gog (Ezek. 38:3).

> c.   That Russia (Rosh) will invade Israel
> in the latter days (Ezek. 38:8).

> d.   That this invasion will be aided by various
> allies of Rosh (Ezek. 38:5, 6), such as

>> (1)   Iran (Persia);
>> (2)   South Africa (Ethiopia);
>> (3)   North Africa (Libya);
>> (4)   Eastern Europe (Gomer);
>> (5)   Southern Russia (Togarmah).

> In Ezekiel 38:15 the prophet describes
> the major part that horses will play
> during this invasion. It is a well-known
> fact that the Cossacks of Southern

Russia have always owned and bred
the largest herd of horses in history!

12. A persecuted woman

"And there appeared a great wonder in heaven:
a woman clothed with the sun, and the moon
under her feet, and upon her head a crown
of twelve stars" (Rev. 12:1). These words
are unquestionably symbolic, but to whom
do they refer?

a. Her identity

(1) She is not Mary. Mary never spent
3½ years in the wilderness, as does
this woman (Rev. 12:6, 14). Neither
was Mary personally hated, chased,
and persecuted, as we see here
(Rev. 12:13, 17). While Mary did give
birth to that One who will someday
"rule all nations with a rod of iron"
(Rev. 12:5), the language in this chapter
has a wider reference than to Mary.
(2) She is not the church. The church
did not bring the manchild into
existence, as does this woman (Rev.
12:5), but rather the opposite!
See Matthew 16:18.
(3) She is Israel. A Jewish Christian
who reads Revelation 12:1 will un-
doubtedly think back to the Old Testament passage in which Joseph describes
a strange dream to his father and eleven
brothers:

"Behold, I have dreamed a dream . . .

the sun and the moon and eleven
stars made obeisance to me"
(Gen. 37:9).

This was of course fulfilled when
Joseph's eleven brothers bowed down
to him in Egypt (Gen. 43:28).
The point of all the above is that the
language of Revelation 12:1 describes
Israel and nothing else!

b. Her activities

(1) This woman (Israel) is hated
by Satan because of
(a) Her historical work of bringing
Christ into the world (Mic. 5:2;
Rev. 12:5, 13);
(b) Her future work of spreading
the gospel to the world (Matt.
24:14; Rev. 7:1-8; 12:17).
(2) This woman is hidden by God
for 3½ years (Rev. 12:6, 14). Some
believe on the basis of Zechariah 13:9
that approximately one-third of the
Israelites living during the awful
Tribulation will escape the wrath
of Satan by fleeing to the ancient city
of Petra.

13. A vile harlot

"One of the seven angels who had poured out
the plagues came over and talked with me.
'Come with me,' he said, 'and I will show you
what is going to happen to the Notorious Prostitute,
who sits upon the many waters of the world.
The kings of the world have had immoral relations

with her, and the people of the earth have been
made drunk by the wine of her immorality.'

"So the angel took me in spirit into the wilderness.
There I saw a woman sitting on a scarlet animal
that had seven heads and ten horns, written
all over with blasphemies against God.
The woman wore purple and scarlet clothing
and beautiful jewelry made of gold and precious
gems and pearls, and held in her hand a golden
goblet full of obscenities.

"A mysterious caption was written on her forehead:
'Babylon the Great, Mother of Prostitutes
and Idol Worship Everywhere around the World.'

"I could see that she was drunk — drunk
with the blood of the martyrs of Jesus she had killed.
I stared at her in horror" (Rev. 17:1-6, TLB).

This brutal, bloody, and blasphemous harlot
is none other than the universal false church,
the wicked wife of Satan! God had no sooner begun
his blessed work in preparing for himself
a people than the Devil did likewise. In fact,
the first baby to be born on this earth later
became Satan's original convert! See Genesis 4:8;
1 John 3:12. We shall now consider the historical,
current, and future activities of this perverted
prostitute.

   a.   The harlot viewed historically

        (1)   Satan's church began officially
        at the tower of Babel in Genesis 11:1-9,
        nearly 24 centuries B.C. Here,
        in the fertile plain of Shinar, probably
        very close to the original Garden of Eden,

the first spade of dirt was turned
for the purpose of Devil-worship.

(2)   The first full-time minister of Satan
was Nimrod, Noah's wicked and
apostate grandson (Gen. 10:8-10).

(3)   Secular history and tradition tell
us that Nimrod married a woman
who was as evil and demonic as himself.
Her name was Semerimus. Knowing
God's promise of a future Savior (Gen.
3:15), Semerimus brazenly claimed
that Tammuz, her first son, fulfilled
this prophecy.

(4)   Semerimus thereupon instituted
a religious system which made both
her and her son the objects of divine
worship. She herself became
the first high priestess. Thus began
the mother-child cult which later spread
all over the world.

>   (a)   From Babylon it spread
>   to Phoenicia under the name of
>   Ashteroth and Tammuz.
>   (b)   From Phoenicia it traveled
>   to Pergamos in Asia Minor. This is
>   the reason for John's admonition
>   to the church at Pergamos
>   in the book of Revelation: "I know
>   thy works, and where thou dwellest,
>   even where Satan's seat is . . ."
>   (Rev. 2:13).
>   (c)   In Egypt the mother-child
>   cult was known as *Isis* and *Horus*.

(d) In Greece it became Aphrodite and *Eros*.

(e) In Rome this pair was worshiped as Venus and Cupid.

Dr. J. Dwight Pentecost writes, "Several years ago I visited an archeological museum in Mexico City. A recent find had just been put on display which Mexican archeologists had authenticated as belonging to the period about 200 years before Christ. The object was the center of religious worship among some of the early Indians in Mexico. To my amazement, it was an image of a mother with a child in her arms. This Babylonian religion spread abroad to become the religion of the world. . . ."[9]

(5) What was the teaching of Semerimus' satanic church?

(a) That Semerimus herself was the way to God. She actually adopted the title "Queen of Heaven."

(b) That she alone could administer salvation to the sinner through various sacraments, such as the sprinkling of holy water.

(c) That her son Tammuz was tragically slain by a wild boar during a hunting trip.

[9]Pentecost, *Prophecy for Today*, p. 133.

(d) That he was, however,
resurrected from the dead forty
days later. Thus, each year
afterward the temple virgins of this
cult would enter a forty-day fast
as a memorial to Tammuz' death
and resurrection.
(e) After the forty-day fast,
a joyful feast called Ishtar took
place. At this feast colored eggs
were exchanged and eaten as a
symbol of the resurrection. An
evergreen tree was displayed and
a yule log was burned. Finally
hot cakes marked with the letter T
(to remind everybody of Tammuz)
were baked and eaten!

(6)   About 2000 B.C. God called
Abraham away from all this (see
Joshua 24:2, 3) and led him into the
Promised Land. But by the ninth
century B.C. Israel had returned
to this devil worship under the influence
of wicked Jezebel (see 1 Kings
16:30-33). At this time the cult was
worshiped under the name of Baal.

(7)   Both Ezekiel and Jeremiah
warned against this hellish thing.
"Then he brought me to the door
of the gate of the Lord's house which
was toward the north; and behold,
there sat women weeping for Tammuz"
(Ezek. 8:14).
"The children gather wood, and the

fathers kindle the fire, and the women
knead their dough, to make cakes
to the queen of heaven . . . to burn
incense to the queen of heaven,
and to pour out drink offerings unto
her . . ." (Jer. 7:18; 44:25).

(8) By the time of Christ this cult
had so influenced Roman life that the
Caesars were not only crowned
as emperors of Rome but also bore
the title *Pontifex Maximus*, meaning,
"high priest." They were high priests
of the Babylonian satanic church!

(9) During the year A.D. 306
a Roman emperor named Constantine
was threatened by a very powerful
enemy army. Realizing that his uneasy
troops needed confidence, Constantine
claimed to have seen a vision on the
eve of the battle. He saw a large blue flag
with a red cross on it and heard
a mighty voice which said *In hoc signo
vinces* — "in this sign conquer." He
thereupon marched his troops into a
shallow river, claimed them to be
officially baptized, and ordered the sign
of the cross painted on all his weapons.
Thus inspired, he led his troops to victory
and subsequently made Christianity
the state religion of Rome.

The Roman priests of Tammuz
soon discovered that they could easily
make the transition into Christianity
(with certain changes) and thereupon

carried their traditions forward without
interruption by promoting the
Madonna-Child worship concept, the
holy water sacrament, etc. For years
the Roman Catholic popes have worn
their well-known "fisherman ring."
This symbol can be traced back
to the Philistines, who worshiped
the fish god Dagon (1 Sam. 5)
along with Tammuz.

Thus for nearly 300 years the Devil
had desperately attempted to destroy
the church from outside by his
terrible persecutions. But with the advent
of Constantine he changed his tactics,
walking the aisle, applying for member-
ship, and joining the church! To this
very day he holds his church letter!
The corrupted church was already
flourishing in Christ's day, and the Savior
delivered a scathing attack against
some of its very deacons and elders!
See Matthew 23.

b. The harlot viewed currently

Is mystery Babylon at work today?
She is indeed, stronger and more sinful
than ever! At least three New Testament
writers describe her latter-day activities
and characteristics.

(1) *Paul*
"This know also, that in the last days
perilous times shall come. For men shall
be lovers of their own selves, covetous,

boasters, proud, blasphemers,
disobedient to parents, unthankful,
unholy, without natural affection,
trucebreakers, false accusers, incontinent,
fierce, despisers of those that are good,
traitors, heady, highminded, lovers
of pleasures more than lovers of God;
having a form of godliness, but denying
the power thereof . . ." (2 Tim. 3:1-5).
"For the time will come when
they will not endure sound doctrine;
but after their own lusts shall they heap
to themselves teachers, having itching
ears; and they shall turn away their ears
from the truth, and shall be turned
unto fables" (2 Tim. 4:3, 4).

(2) *Peter*
"But there were false prophets also
among the people, even as there
shall be false teachers among you,
who privily shall bring in damnable
heresies, even denying the Lord
that bought them . . ." (2 Pet. 2:1).

(3) *John*
"I know thy works, that thou art
neither cold nor hot; I would thou wert
cold or hot. So then because thou art
lukewarm, and neither cold nor hot,
I will spue thee out of my mouth.
Because thou sayest, I am rich and
increased with goods, and have need
of nothing, and knowest not that thou art
wretched, and miserable, and poor,
and blind, and naked" (Rev. 3:15-17).

c. The harlot viewed prophetically

What will the future hold for this vile and
vicious vixen? According to Revelation 17
the false church lends all her evil strength
to elevate the antichrist during the first part
of the Tribulation. For awhile she flourishes,
luxuriating in surpassing wealth and opulence.
But suddenly things change drastically.
John describes this for us:

"The scarlet animal and his ten horns —
which represent ten kings who will reign
with him — all hate the woman, and will
attack her and leave her naked and ravaged
by fire" (Rev. 17:16).

The probable reason for all this is that after
she has put the antichrist into power,
the harlot then attempts to control him.
But he won't bow! Thus the world
will finally be rid of the most deadly and
despicable woman who ever lived!

14. An arrogant queen

"After all this I saw another angel come down
from heaven with great authority, and the earth
grew bright with his splendor.

"He gave a mighty shout, 'Babylon the Great
is fallen, is fallen; she has become a den
of demons, a haunt of devils and every kind
of evil spirit. For all the nations have drunk
the fatal wine of her intense immorality. The rulers
of earth have enjoyed themselves with her,
and businessmen throughout the world
have grown rich from all her luxurious living.'

"Then I heard another voice calling from heaven,
'Come away from her, my people; do not take part
in her sins, or you will be punished with her.
For her sins are piled as high as heaven and
God is ready to judge her for her crimes.
Do to her as she has done to you, and more —
give double penalty for all her evil deeds.
She brewed many a cup of woe for others — give
twice as much to her. She has lived in luxury
and pleasure — match it now with torments
and with sorrows. She boasts, "I am queen
upon my throne. I am no helpless widow.
I will not experience sorrow" ' " (Rev. 18:1-7, TLB).

In his excellent commentary on the Book of
Revelation, Dr. J. Vernon McGee writes,

"In chapters 17 and 18 two Babylons are brought
before us. The Babylon of chapter 17 is
ecclesiastical. The Babylon of chapter 18
is economic. The first is religious — the apostate
church. The second is political and commercial.
The apostate church is hated by the kings
of the earth (Rev. 17:16); the commercial center
is loved by the kings of the earth (Rev. 18:9).
The apostate church is destroyed by the kings
of the earth; political Babylon is destroyed
by the judgment of God (verses 5, 8).
Obviously, mystery Babylon is destroyed first —
in the midst of the Great Tribulation;
while commercial Babylon is destroyed
at the Second Coming of Christ. These two
Babylons are not one and the same city."[10]

We shall now trace economic and political Babylon
through a twofold outline.

---

[10]J. Vernon McGee, *Reveling through Revelation* (Pasadena: Thru the Bible
Radio Foundation), p. 58. Used by permission.

a. The location of the city

Is this city a literal one? Of that there seems
to be no doubt. It is an actual, literal city
which will outshine all other cities during
the Tribulation and doubtless also
serve as headquarters for the antichrist.
Will ancient Babylon actually be rebuilt
on the Euphrates, as in Daniel's time?
Some believe it will, for the following reasons:

(1) Ancient Babylon was never
suddenly destroyed, as prophesied in
Isaiah 13:19.

(2) The description of literal Babylon
by Jeremiah in chapter 51 is very
similar to the one given by John
in Revelation 18.

(3) Babylon is said to be destroyed
during the day of the Lord, which is
an Old Testament term referring
to the Tribulation. See Isaiah 13:6.

(4) According to Isaiah 14 Israel will
enter into God's rest after Babylon
is destroyed. Since this has not
yet happened, the event must be still
future.

(5) Archaeological discoveries have
shown that bricks and stones from
ancient Babylon have been re-used
for building purposes, contrary to the
prophecy of Jeremiah 51:26.

(6) Jeremiah predicts (25:17-26)
that Babylon will drink of the cup of the
wrath of God *last* among all the
kingdoms of the earth.

(7) The vision of the woman in the ephah (Zech. 5:5-11) indicates a return of wickedness and commerce to Babylon.

(8) The description in Revelation 18 is best understood if taken literally.

This list is derived from *Bible Prophecy Notes,* by R. Ludwigson.

Dr. McGee (who believes Babylon will be literally rebuilt) quotes from the following news item, which appeared in July 1962. He does not mention the source of this clipping.

"According to an announcement of the ministry of Antiquities in Bagdad, the Tower of Babel is to be rebuilt. Although it will not 'reach unto heaven,' as its original builders intended, it will nevertheless provide the tourists with a splendid observation tower more than 300 feet high. From this height, the sight-seers will have a panoramic view of the site of ancient Babylon. The reconstruction of the Tower of Babel will be carried out — as far as possible — according to the original dimensions found in ancient documents.

"The first tower is supposed to have had a base of nearly 300,000 square feet and have been erected about seventy miles south of Babylon. . . . After completion of the Tower of Babel, the Iraqi ministry for Antiquities intends to hold an annual festival, the focal point of which will be the new tower."

b. The description of the city

> (1) It had become the habitation of
> demons and false doctrines (Rev. 18:2;
> Matt. 13:32).
> (2) Both rulers and merchants
> had worshiped at her shrine of silver
> (Rev. 18:3).
> (3) Her sins had reached into the
> heavens (Rev. 18:5).
> (4) She had lived in sinful pleasure
> and luxury (Rev. 18:7).
> (5) Her prosperity had blinded her
> to the judgment of God (Rev. 18:7).

There is in this chapter a list (Rev. 18:11-17)
of no less than twenty-five of the world's
most expensive luxury items. Again the words
of J. Vernon McGee are revealing here:

"Everything listed here is a luxury item.
Babylon will make these luxury items neces-
sities. You will not find a cotton dress
or a pair of overalls anywhere in this list.
First there is the jewelry department —
'. . . the merchandise of gold, and silver,
and precious stones, and of pearls. . . .'
Then we move from the jewelry department
to the ladies' ready-to-wear —
'. . . and fine linen, and purple, and silk,
and scarlet';
Then to the luxury gift department —
'. . . and all thyine wood, and every vessel
of ivory, and every vessel made of most
precious wood, and of brass, and iron,
and marble';

We move on to the spice and cosmetic
department —
    '. . . and cinnamon, and spice, and odors,
    and ointment, and frankincense,'
To the liquor department and the pastry
center —
    '. . . and wine, and oil, and fine flour, and
    wheat . . .'
On to the meat department for T-bone steaks
and lamb chops —
    '. . . and cattle, and sheep.' "[11]

> (6) She had deceived all nations
> with her sorceries (Rev. 18:23).
> (7) She was covered with the blood
> of many of God's saints (Rev. 18:24).

15. A Pure Bride

"Let us be glad and rejoice, and give honour to him,
for the marriage of the Lamb is come, and his wife
hath made herself ready. And to her was granted
that she should be arrayed in fine linen, clean
and white; for the fine linen is the righteousness
of saints" (Rev. 19:7, 8).

This is, of course, a description of the church,
which is composed of all believers saved
from Pentecost to the Rapture! See
2 Corinthians 11:2; Ephesians 5:23-32.

16. A mighty warrior from heaven —

"And I saw heaven opened, and behold,
a white horse; and he that sat upon him was called
Faithful and True, and in righteousness he doth judge

---

[11]McGee, *Reveling through Revelation,* pp. 62, 63.

and make war. His eyes were as a flame of fire, and on his head were many crowns; and he had a name written that no man knew but he himself.

"And he was clothed with a vesture dipped in blood; and his name is called The Word of God. And the armies which were in heaven followed him upon white horses, clothed in fine linen, white and clean.

"And out of his mouth goeth a sharp sword, that with it he should smite the nations; and he shall rule them with a rod of iron; and he treadeth the winepress of the fierceness and wrath of Almighty God.

"And he hath on his vesture and on his thigh a name written: KING OF KINGS AND LORD OF LORDS" (Rev. 19:11-16).

   a. His identity

There is absolutely no doubt whatsoever as to whom these words refer. No angel in heaven, no soldier on earth, no demon in hell could even remotely fill this description! This heavenly warrior is the Lord Jesus Christ himself!

   b. His names and titles
          (1) Faithful and True
          (2) The Word of God
          (3) The King of Kings
          (4) The Lord of Lords
          (5) A name known only to himself

   c. His purpose for coming
          (1) To smite the nations;

(2) To judge the nations;
(3) To rule the nations.

One other passage in Revelation describes this breathtaking event:

"And the seventh angel sounded; and there were great voices in heaven, saying, The kingdoms of this world are become the kingdoms of our Lord, and of his Christ; and he shall reign forever and ever.

"And the four and twenty elders which sat before God on their seats fell upon their faces and worshiped God, saying, We give thee thanks, O Lord God Almighty, which art, and wast, and art to come; because thou hast taken to thee thy great power, and hast reigned. And the nations were angry, and thy wrath is come, and the time of the dead, that they should be judged, and that thou shouldest give reward unto thy servants the prophets, and to the saints, and them that fear thy name, small and great; and shouldest destroy them which destroy the earth" (Rev. 11:15-18).

P. The Chronology of the Tribulation

We have examined very briefly the sixteen main *actors* of the Tribulation; now we turn our attention to the *action* of this seven-year period.

The First Half of the Tribulation (3½ years)

1. The formal organization of the super harlot church

It is composed of apostate masses from Protestantism, Catholicism, Judaisim, and every other major world religion. It is entirely possible that the World Council of Churches will spearhead this latter-day ungodly union. A recent event would strongly suggest this. In 1955, as a celebration of the tenth anniversary of the United Nations, a special "Festival of Faith" was held in the San Francisco Cow Palace. This was reported in the September issue of *The National Council Outlook,* the official organ of the National Council of Churches. Here are their own words:

"Today in the United Nations mankind finds new hope for the achievement of peace.

"This hope was given dramatic expression last June 19 when some 16,000 persons of every race, creed, and color assembled in San Francisco's Cow Palace to pray for peace and pledge their support to the United Nations. . . .

"There were Christians and Jews, Buddhists and Confucianists, Hindus and Moslems — men whose names are household words around the world, and workaday folk.

"They called God by different names — speaking to Him in different tongues, but the dream for peace in their hearts was the same — and the prayers on their lips echoed the prayers of people around the world. Initiated by the San Francisco Council of Churches, the Festival of Faith was a symbol for all men of the oneness of their aspirations. . . . High point of the prayer meeting was the recitation together of the Responsive Reading, composed of sentences from the sacred books of the six faiths represented —

Christian, Jewish, Moslem, Buddhist, Hindu,
and Confucian."

2. The appearance of the antichrist and his
false prophet

We have already observed a number of things
about this perverted pair from the pit.
See Daniel 7:19-25; 11:36-45; 2 Thessalonians
2:1-12; Revelation 13. It is entirely possible
that the antichrist will come from the United Nations,
while the false prophet may well proceed
from the World Council of Churches.

It is also entirely feasible that both personages
are alive and active in this world right now,
and are waiting for the Rapture to remove the
final barrier, thus allowing them to begin
their deadly and damnable work!

3. The Revival of the Roman Empire (Dan. 2:41;
7:7, 8; Rev. 13:1; 17:12)

During his Olivet Discourse our Lord uttered the
following sober sentence concerning Jerusalem.
It was both historical and prophetical in its scope.
He proclaimed:

". . . and Jerusalem shall be trodden down
of the Gentiles, until the times of the Gentiles
be fulfilled" (Luke 21:24).

Concerning this Scofield observes,

"The 'times of the Gentiles' began with the captivity
of Judah under Nebuchadnezzar (2 Chron.
36:1-21), since which time Jerusalem has been
under Gentile overlordship" (*Scofield Bible,*
p. 1106).

Both the history and the prophecy of Christ's
statement are taken from two chapters in the
Book of Daniel. In chapter 2 God reveals these
"times of the Gentiles" to a Babylonian king
and in chapter 7 he reveals his great secret
to Daniel himself. We now note the following:

a. This period as seen by Nebuchadnezzar

"O king, you saw a huge and powerful statue
of a man, shining brilliantly, frightening
and terrible. The head of the statue was made
of purest gold, its chest and arms were
of silver, its belly and thighs of brass,
its legs of iron, its feet part iron and part clay.
But as you watched, a Rock was cut
from the mountainside by supernatural means.
It came hurtling toward the statue
and crushed the feet of iron and clay,
smashing them to bits. Then the whole statue
collapsed into a heap of iron, clay, brass,
silver, and gold; its pieces were crushed
as small as chaff, and the wind blew
them all away. But the Rock that knocked
the statue down became a great mountain
that covered the whole earth.

"That was the dream; now for its meaning:

"Your Majesty, you are a king over many
kings, for the God of heaven has given you
your kingdom, power, strength and glory.
You rule the farthest provinces, and even
animals and birds are under your control,
as God decreed. You are that head of gold.

"But after your kingdom has come to an end,
another world power will arise to take your

place. This empire will be inferior to yours.
And after that kingdom has fallen, yet a third
great power — represented by the bronze
belly of the statue — will rise to rule
the world. Following it, the fourth kingdom
will be strong as iron — smashing, bruising,
and conquering. The feet and toes you saw
— part iron and part clay — show that later on
this kingdom will be divided. Some parts
of it will be as strong as iron and some
as weak as clay. This mixture of iron
with clay also shows that these kingdoms
will try to strengthen themselves by forming
alliances with each other through intermarriage
of their rulers; but this will not succeed,
for iron and clay don't mix.

"During the reigns of those kings the God
of heaven will set up a kingdom that will
never be destroyed; no one will ever conquer
it. It will shatter all these kingdoms
into nothingness, but it shall stand forever,
indestructible. That is the meaning of the Rock
cut from the mountain without human
hands — the Rock that crushed to powder
all the iron and brass, the clay, the silver,
and the gold.

"Thus the great God has shown what will
happen in the future, and this interpretation
of your dream is as sure and certain as
my description of it" (Dan. 2:31-45, TLB).

b. This period as seen by Daniel

"One night during the first year of Belshazzar's
reign over the Babylonian empire,

Daniel had a dream and he wrote it down.
This is his description of what he saw:

"In my dream I saw a great storm on
a mighty ocean, with strong winds blowing
from every direction. Then four huge animals
came up out of the water, each different
from the other. The first was like a lion,
but it had eagle's wings! And as I watched,
its wings were pulled off so that it could
no longer fly, and it was left standing
on the ground, on two feet, like a man;
and a man's mind was given to it. The second
animal looked like a bear with its paw raised,
ready to strike. It held three ribs between
its teeth, and I heard a voice saying to it,
'Get up! Devour many people!' The third
of these strange animals looked like
a leopard, but on its back it had wings
like those of birds, and it had four heads!
And great power was given to it over all
mankind.

"Then, as I watched in my dream, a fourth
animal rose up out of the ocean, too dreadful
to describe and incredibly strong. It
devoured some of its victims by tearing them
apart with its huge iron teeth, and others
it crushed beneath its feet. It was far more
brutal and vicious than any of the other
animals, and it had ten horns.

"As I was looking at the horns, suddenly
another small horn appeared among them,
and three of the first ones were yanked out,
roots and all, to give it room; this little horn
had a man's eyes and a bragging mouth.

"I watched as thrones were put in place
and the Ancient of Days — the Almighty God
— sat down to judge. His clothing was as
white as snow, his hair like whitest wool.
He sat upon a fiery throne brought in
on flaming wheels, and a river of fire flowed
from before him. Millions of angels
ministered to him and hundreds of millions
of people stood before him, waiting to be
judged. Then the court began its session
and The Books were opened.

"As I watched, the brutal fourth animal
was killed and its body handed over to be
burned because of its arrogance against
Almighty God, and the boasting of its little
horn. As for the other three animals,
their kingdoms were taken from them,
but they were allowed to live a short time
longer.

"Next I saw the arrival of a Man — or so
he seemed to be — brought there on clouds
from heaven; he approached the Ancient
of Days and was presented to him. He
was given the ruling power and glory
over all the nations of the world, so that all
people of every language must obey him.
His power is eternal — it will never end;
his government shall never fall.

"I was confused and disturbed by all
I had seen (Daniel wrote in his report), so I
approached one of those standing beside
the throne and asked him the meaning
of all these things, and he explained them
to me.

" 'These four huge animals,' he said,
'represent four kings who will someday rule
the earth. But in the end the people of the
Most High God shall rule the governments
of the world forever and forever.'

"Then I asked about the fourth animal,
the one so brutal and shocking, with its iron
teeth and brass claws that tore men apart
and that stamped others to death with its feet.
I asked, too, about the ten horns and
the little horn that came up afterward
and destroyed three of the others — the horn
with the eyes, and the loud, bragging mouth,
the one which was stronger than the others.
For I had seen this horn warring against
God's people and winning, until the Ancient
of Days came and opened his court and
vindicated his people, giving them worldwide
powers of government.

" 'This fourth animal,' he told me, 'is the fourth
world power that will rule the earth.
It will be more brutal than any of the others;
it will devour the whole world, destroying
everything before it. His ten horns
are ten kings that will rise out of his empire;
then another king will arise, more brutal
than the other ten, and will destroy three
of them. He will defy the Most High God,
and wear down the saints with persecution,
and try to change all laws, morals, and
customs. God's people will be helpless
in his hands for three and a half years.

" 'But then the Ancient of Days will come
and open his court of justice and take all

power from this vicious king, to consume
and destroy it until the end. Then every
nation under heaven, and all their power,
shall be given to the people of God;
they shall rule all things forever, and all
rulers shall serve and obey them' "
(Dan. 7:1-27, TLB).

From these two extended passages and from
secular history we learn that —

a. Four major powers (or kingdoms)
will rule over Palestine.

b. These powers are viewed by mankind
as gold, silver, brass, iron, and clay.

c. These powers are viewed by God
as four wild animals: a winged lion, a bear,
a winged leopard, and an indescribably
brutal and vicious animal.

d. These four powers stand for

(1) Babylon — from 625 B.C. to
539 B.C.;

(2) Medo-Persia — from 539 B.C.
to 331 B.C.;

(3) Greece — from 331 B.C. to
323 B.C.;

(4) Rome — three periods are to be
noted here:

(a) The first period — the
original empire — from 300 B.C.
to A.D. 476

(b) The second period — the intervening influence — from A.D. 476 to the present.

We are amazed at Rome's continuing world influence centuries after the official collapse of its empire. As Erich Sauer observes,

"The Roman *administration* lives on in the Church of Rome. The ecclesiastical provinces coincided with the State provinces; and Rome, the chief city of the world empire, became the chief city of the world church, the seat of the Papacy.

"The Roman *tongue* lives on in the Latin of the Church, and is still in use in the international technical language of law, medicine, and natural science.

"Roman *law* lives on in legislation. The Corpus Juris Romanum (body of Roman law) of the Eastern Roman Emperor Justinian (A.D. 527-565) became the foundation of jurisprudence among the Latin and Germanic peoples throughout the Middle Ages and far into Modern times.

"The Roman *army* lives on in military systems. It became the model for armaments and western defence. We still use Latin words such as captain, major,

general, battalion, regiment, army,
infantry, artillery, and cavalry."[12]
(c) The third period — the
Revived Empire — from the Rapture to Armageddon

e. This Revived Roman Empire will consist
of ten nations.

f. The antichrist will personally unite
these western nations.

One has only to consult his newspaper in order
to follow the rapid present-day fulfillment of this
revived Roman Empire prophecy! Students of
history will readily agree that the unity of any empire
of nations depends upon four factors. These are
the military, the economic, the political, and
the religious. With this mind, consider the following
recent developments in Western Europe:

a. The military aspect

On April 4, 1949, the North Atlantic Treaty
Organization (NATO) was formally
brought into being.

b. The economic aspect

On June 23, 1971, at 5:00 A.M.,
champagne was served in Luxembourg.
A historical treaty had finally been concluded
by British Prime Minister Edward Heath
and French President Georges Pompidou.
The long-coveted European Common Market
was now a reality! This market, representing

---

[12]Erich Sauer, *The Triumph of the Crucified* (Grand Rapids: Eerdmans, 1951), p. 132.

260 million people, *is composed of ten nations!*
These are:

France	Belgium
Italy	Luxembourg
The Netherlands	Denmark
Great Britain	Norway
West Germany	Ireland

c. The political aspect

This will be brought into being by the
antichrist.

d. The religious aspect

This will be brought into being by the false
prophet.

We conclude this section with a quotation from
Dr. Donald Barnhouse:

"Many men have been haunted with the idea
of a revival of this empire, but it has never yet
been revived. Charlemagne attempted it, and the
pope who crowned him Emperor on Christmas Day
of the year 800 no doubt saw a revival of Caesar's
power. But at Charlemagne's death the dream
vanished, and the division of his kingdom at
the treaty of Verdun in 843 laid the foundation
for all the wars of Western Europe since that time.
The Holy Roman Empire was then established,
and it moved in spectral fashion across the history
of the centuries that followed — never achieved,
yet never forgotten. Napoleon found himself on an
island in the South Atlantic after he had
consolidated European power for a few brief
moments and named his own little boy 'the king

of Rome.' Mussolini added a worthless African
plateau to the territory of Rome and immediately
proclaimed a 'Roman Empire,' a haunting name,
evoking thoughts of grandeur and glory that have
never been forgotten since the Roman legions
wrote their laws in letters of blood across the
Mediterranean lands. But the death stroke of the
Roman Empire most certainly will be healed.
God's Word will never pass away. Every jot and
tittle must be fulfilled."[13]

4. The antichrist's seven-year covenant with Israel

"And your covenant with death shall be disannulled,
and your agreement with hell shall not stand"
(Isaiah 28:18).
"And he shall confirm the covenant with many
for one week . . ." (Dan. 9:27).

a. The background of the covenant

From June 4 through June 8, 1967,
the world-famous six-day war between Israel
and Egypt took place. When the smoke
had cleared, Israel had won a stunning
and fantastic victory! Her land area had
increased from 7,992 square miles to over
26,000 square miles. With less than 50,000
troops she had all but annihilated Nasser's
90,000 soldiers. During that fateful week
Egypt suffered 30,000 casualties, 197 planes,
700 tanks, and watched two billion dollars
go up in smoke! Israel, on the other hand,
lost 61 tanks, 275 dead, and 800 wounded.
But in spite of all this, Israel's position

[13]Barnhouse, *Revelation*, pp. 237, 238.

in Palestine today is anything but secure!
She continues to find herself surrounded
by powerful enemies who have sworn
by their gods to drive her into the sea.
In addition to this her northern neighbor,
Soviet Russia, views her land with growing
interest.

The Word of God indicates that this already-
intolerable situation will worsen. Then
(shortly after the Rapture), to her astonishment and relief, a powerful Western leader
(the antichrist) will pretend to befriend Israel.
In fact, he will propose a special seven-year
security treaty, guaranteeing to maintain
the status quo in the Middle East. Israel
will swallow this poisoned bait, hook,
line, and sinker!

Before proceeding to the next section, two
recent events may be noted which tend
to illuminate this coming seven-year covenant.

> (1) In May of 1971, a 15-year alliance
> pact was formed between Cairo
> and Moscow!
> (2) On June 19, 1970, the U.S.
> Secretary of State, William P. Rogers,
> visited Israel in an attempt to settle
> the Middle East crisis.

The point of the above dates is that during
the Tribulation two important alliances will be
formed in the Middle East. One is between
Israel and the Western Antichrist. The other
is between Russia and Egypt. Thus even
today we hear the distant thunder of the
approaching tribulational storm!

b. The betrayal of the covenant

"This king will make a seven-year treaty
with the people, but after half that time,
he will break his pledge and stop the Jews
from all their sacrifice and their offerings;
then, as a climax to all his terrible deeds,
the Enemy shall utterly defile the sanctuary
of God . . ." (Dan. 9:27, TLB).

5. The pouring out of the first six seals
(Rev. 6:1-17; Matt. 24:4-8)

"And I saw in the right hand of him that sat
on the throne a book written within and on the
backside, sealed with seven seals" (Rev. 5:1).
"And I saw when the Lamb opened one of the seals,
and I heard as it were the noise of thunder . . ."
(Rev. 6:1).

a. The first seal (Rev. 6:2)

"And I saw, and behold, a white horse;
and he that sat on him had a bow; and a crown
was given unto him; and he went forth
conquering, and to conquer."

This is doubtless a symbolic picture of the
antichrist as he subdues to himself the ten
nations of the revived Roman Empire.
This may be thought of as the "cold war"
period.

b. The second seal (Rev. 6:3, 4)

"And when he had opened the second seal,
I heard the second beast say, Come and see.
And there went out another horse that was red;
and power was given to him that sat

thereon to take peace from the earth,
and that they should kill one another;
and there was given unto him a great sword."

The uneasy peace which the rider
on the white horse brings to earth is temporary
and counterfeit. The antichrist promises peace,
but only God can actually produce it!
As Isaiah would write, "But the wicked
are like the troubled sea, when it cannot rest,
whose waters cast up mire and dirt.
There is no peace, saith my God,
to the wicked" (Isa. 57:20, 21).

Now open and bloody hostility breaks out
among some of the nations.

c. The third seal (Rev. 6:5, 6)

"And when he had opened the third seal,
I heard the third beast say, Come and see.
And I beheld, and lo, a black horse;
and he that sat on him had a pair of balances
in his hand. And I heard a voice in the midst
of the four beasts say, A measure of wheat
for a penny, and three measures of barley
for a penny; and see thou hurt not the oil
and the wine."

Dr. Charles Ryrie writes the following
concerning this seal:

"The third judgment brings famine to the
world. The black horse forebodes death,
and the pair of balances bespeaks a careful
rationing of food. Normally, a 'penny'
(a Roman denarius, a day's wages in Palestine
in Jesus' day, Matt. 20:2) would buy eight
measures of wheat or twenty-four of barley.

Under these famine conditions the same wage
will buy only one measure of wheat
or three of barley. In other words,
there will be one-eighth of the normal
supply of food. The phrase 'see thou hurt
not the oil and the wine' is an ironic twist
in this terrible situation. Apparently
luxury food items will not be in short supply,
but of course most people will not be able
to afford them. This situation will only serve
to taunt the populace in their impoverished
state."[14]

Will the food problem really be as bad as all
this during the Tribulation? One of the
best-selling books of the late sixties
was titled *The Population Bomb,*
and was written by Stanford University
biology professor Dr. Paul R. Ehrlich.
The following are but a few of the frightening
quotes from his pen:

"While you are reading these words
four people will have died from starvation,
most of them children" (from the cover).

"The battle to feed all of humanity is over.
In the 1970's the world will undergo famines
— hundreds of millions of people are going
to starve to death in spite of any crash programs embarked upon now" (from
the Prologue).

"The rich are going to get richer,
but the more numerous poor are going
to get poorer. Of these poor, a minimum

---

[14]Charles Ryrie, *Revelation* (Chicago: Moody, 1968), pp. 45, 46. Used by permission.

of three and one-half million will starve
to death this year, mostly children. But this is
a mere handful compared to the numbers
that will be starving in a decade or so."[15]

d. The fourth seal (Rev. 6:7, 8)

"And when he had opened the fourth seal,
I heard the voice of the fourth beast say,
Come and see. And I looked, and behold
a pale horse; and his name that sat on him
was Death, and Hell followed with him.
And power was given unto them over the
fourth part of the earth, to kill with sword,
and with hunger, and with death,
and with the beasts of the earth."

(1) The identity of these riders
John calls them "death" and "hell,"
apparently referring to physical
and spiritual death. Thus the Devil
will destroy the bodies and damn the
souls of multitudes of unbelievers
during this third seal plague.

(2) The damage done by these riders
One-fourth of all humanity perishes
during this plague! It is estimated
that during the Second World War one
out of forty persons lost their lives,
but this seal judgment alone will claim
one out of four persons — nearly
one billion human beings!

e. The fifth seal (Rev. 6:9-11)

"And when he had opened the fifth seal,

[15]Paul R. Ehrlich, *The Population Bomb* (San Francisco: Sierra, 1969), p. 17.

I saw under the altar the souls of them
that were slain for the word of God,
and for the testimony which they held;
and they cried with a loud voice,
saying, How long, O Lord, holy and true,
dost thou not judge and avenge our blood
on them that dwell on the earth? And white
robes were given unto every one of them;
and it was said unto them that they should
rest yet for a little season, until their fellow-
servants also and their brethren, that should
be killed as they were, should be fulfilled."

These three verses are loaded with theological
implications.

(1) They refute the damnable doctrine
of soul sleep!

(2) They correct the error of one
general resurrection.

It is evident that these martyred souls
did not receive their glorified bodies
at the Rapture, as did the church-age
saints. Therefore it can be concluded
these are Old Testament saints who will
experience the glorious bodily resurrection
after the Tribulation. See Revelation
20:4-6.

(3) They suggest the possibilities of
an intermediate body.
Dr. John Walvoord writes,

"The martyred dead here pictured
have not been raised from the dead
and have not received their resurrection
bodies. Yet it is declared that they are

given robes. The fact that they are given
robes would almost demand that they
have a body of some sort. A robe
could not hang upon an immaterial soul
or spirit. It is not the kind of body
that Christians now have, that is,
the body of earth; nor is it the resurrection body of flesh and bones of which
Christ spoke after His own resurrection.
It is a temporary body suited for their
presence in heaven but replaced
in turn by their everlasting resurrection
body given at the time of Christ's
return."[16]

f. The sixth seal (Rev. 6:12-17)

"And I beheld when he had opened the
sixth seal, and lo, there was a great earthquake;
and the sun became black as sackcloth
of hair, and the moon became as blood;
and the stars of heaven fell unto the earth,
even as a fig tree casteth her untimely figs
when she is shaken of a mighty wind.
And the heaven departed as a scroll
when it is rolled together; and every mountain
and island were moved out of their places.

"And the kings of the earth, and the great men,
and the rich men, and the chief captains,
and the mighty men, and every bondman,
and every free man, hid themselves in the dens
and in the rocks, of the mountains, and said
to the mountains and rocks, Fall on us,
and hide us from the face of him that

---

[16]Walvoord, *The Revelation of Jesus Christ*, pp. 134, 135.

sitteth on the throne, and from the wrath
of the Lamb; for the great day of his wrath
is come, and who shall be able to stand?"

6. The mass return of the Jews to Palestine

One of the most remarkable chapters in all the Bible
concerns itself with the latter-day return of the Jews
to Palestine.

"The power of the Lord was upon me and I was
carried away by the Spirit of the Lord to a valley
full of old, dry bones that were scattered
everywhere across the ground. He led me
around among them, and then he said to me:

" 'Son of dust, can these bones become people
again?'

"I replied, 'Lord, you alone know the answer to that.'

"Then he told me to speak to the bones and say:
'O dry bones, listen to the words of God,
for the Lord God says, See! I am going to make you
live and breathe again! I will replace the flesh
and muscles on you and cover you with skin.
I will put breath into you, and you shall live
and know I am the Lord.'

"So I spoke these words from God, just as he told
me to; and suddenly there was a rattling noise
from all across the valley, and the bones of each
body came together and attached to each other
as they used to be. Then, as I watched,
the muscles and flesh formed over the bones,
and skin covered them, but the bodies had
no breath. Then he told me to call to the wind
and say: 'The Lord God says: Come from
the four winds, O Spirit, and breathe upon these

slain bodies, that they may live again.' So I spoke
to the winds as he commanded me and the bodies
began breathing; they lived, and stood up —
a very great army.

"Then he told me what the vision meant:
'These bones,' he said, 'represent all the people
of Israel. They say: We have become a heap
of dried-out bones — all hope is gone. But tell them,
the Lord God says: My people, I will open
your graves of exile and cause you to rise again
and return to the land of Israel. And, then at last,
O my people, you will know I am the Lord.
I will put my Spirit into you, and you shall live
and return home again to your own land. Then
you will know that I, the Lord, have done
just what I promised you' " (Ezek. 37:1-14, TLB).

Even today we see the beginning of this future
Israelite ingathering. Note the following figures:

> In 1882 there were approximately 25,000
> Jews in Palestine.
> In 1900 there were 50,000.
> In 1922 there were 84,000.
> In 1931 there were 175,000.
> In 1948 there were 650,000.
> In 1952 there were 1,421,000.
> Today there are approximately 3,000,000
> Jews in Palestine.

Thus the number of Jews has increased nearly
120 times in less than 95 years! They have been
gathered from over one hundred countries.
Three additional passages bear out this latter-day
Jewish return:

"For thus saith the Lord God, Behold, I, even I,
will both search my sheep and seek them out.

As a shepherd seeketh out his flock in the day
that he is among his sheep that are scattered,
so will I seek out my sheep, and will deliver them
out of all places where they have been scattered
in the cloudy and dark day. And I will bring
them out from the people, and gather them
from the countries, and will bring them
to their own land . . ." (Ezek. 34:11-13).
"For I will take you from among the heathen,
and gather you out of all countries, and will bring
you into your own land" (Ezek. 36:24).
"Fear not, for I am with thee; I will bring thy seed
from the east and gather thee from the west;
I will say to the north, Give up; and to the south,
Keep not back: bring my sons from far,
and my daughters from the ends of the earth"
(Isa. 43:5, 6).

7. The conversion and call of the 144,000
(Rev. 7:1-4)

"And after these things I saw four angels standing
on the four corners of the earth, holding
the four winds of the earth, that the wind should not
blow on the earth, nor on the sea, nor on any tree.
And I saw another angel ascending from the east,
having the seal of the Living God; and he cried
with a loud voice to the four angels, to whom
it was given to hurt the earth and the sea,
saying, Hurt not the earth, neither the sea,
nor the trees, till we have sealed the servants
of our God in their foreheads. And I heard
the number of them which were sealed; and there
were sealed an hundred and forty and four thousand
of all the tribes of the children of Israel."

This passage does not mean that God will save

only Jews during the Tribulation, for in
Revelation 7:9-17 the Bible declares that
a great multitude from every nation will be saved.
What this chapter does teach, however, is that God
will send out 144,000 "Hebrew Billy Sundays"
to evangelize the world! This will be a massive
number indeed, especially when we consider
that there are less than 35,000 missionaries of all
persuasions in the world today!

Our Lord doubtless had the ministry of the 144,000
in mind when he said,

"And this gospel of the kingdom shall be
preached in all the world for a witness unto
all nations; and then shall the end come"
(Matt. 24:14).

8. The rebuilding of the Jewish temple

There is ample scriptural evidence to show
that the antichrist will allow (and perhaps
even encourage) the building of the temple and
the rendering of its sacrifices during the Tribulation.
See Daniel 9:27; 12:11; Matthew 24:15;
2 Thessalonians 2:4; Revelation 13:14, 15; 11:2.

In his book *Will Man Survive?*, Dr. J. D. Pentecost
quotes from a Jewish ad that appeared
in the Washington Post during May, 1967.

"A project to rebuild the temple of God in Israel
is now being started. With divine help
and guidance the temple will be completed. It will
signal a new era in Judaism. Jews will be inspired
to conduct themselves in such a moral way
that our maker will see fit to pay us a visit here
on the earth. Imagine the warm feelings that
will be ours when this happy event takes place."

9. The ministry of the two witnesses (Rev. 11:3-13)

   a. Their identity

   As we have already seen, a number of scholars believe these two are Moses and Elijah.

   b. Their ministry

   > (1) To prophesy in sackcloth before men as God's anointed lampstands.
   > (2) To destroy their enemies in the same manner that their enemies would attempt to destroy them.
   > (3) To prevent rain for 3½ years.
   > (4) To turn waters into blood.
   > (5) To smite the earth with every kind of plague.

   c. Their death

   > (1) The antichrist is finally allowed to kill them.
   > (2) To show his contempt for them, he refuses to permit their dead bodies to be buried, but leaves them to rot in the streets of Jerusalem.
   > (3) All the earth celebrates their deaths through a hellish Christmas; men actually send gifts to each other!
   > (4) The dead bodies of these two prophets are viewed by all the nations of the world in a 3½ day period.

   It is interesting to note that this prophecy (Rev. 11:9) could not have been fulfilled until the middle sixties. The following article explains why:

"The first link in a worldwide, live television
system was taken on May 2, 1965, when the
Early Bird Satellite, hovering 22,300
miles in space between Brazil and Africa,
united millions of American and European
viewers in an international television
exchange" (*Reader's Digest Almanac,* 1966
edition).

d. Their resurrection (here the word "great"
appears three times)

(1) A great voice calls them up
to heaven (Rev. 11:12).
(2) A great fear falls upon those
who witness this (Rev. 11:11).
(3) A great earthquake levels
one-tenth of Jerusalem and kills 7000
prominent men (Rev. 11:13).

The Middle Segment of the Tribulation (a brief undetermined period)

We have already suggested that the seven-year Tribulation
may be broken up into three sections. The first part
is 3½ years, the middle perhaps just a few days,
and the last again 3½ years. We shall now observe
six important events which may, with some degree
of certainty, be placed in this brief middle period.

1. The Gog and Magog invasion into Palestine
(Ezek. 38, 39)

"Son of man, set thy face toward Gog, of the land
of Magog, the prince of Rosh, Meshech, and Tubal,
and prophecy against him, and say, thus saith
the Lord Jehovah; Behold, I am against thee,

O Gog, prince of Rosh, Meshech, and Tubal . . ."
(Ezek. 38:2, 3, *American Standard Version,* 1901).

a. The identity of the invaders

Where is the land of Magog? It seems
almost certain that these verses in Ezekiel
refer to none other than that Red Communistic
bear, the U.S.S.R. Note the following
threefold proof of this.

(1) Geographical proof
Ezekiel tells us in three distinct passages
(38:6, 15; 39:2) that this invading
nation will come from the "uttermost
parts of the north" (as the original
Hebrew renders it). A quick glance
at any world map will show that only
Russia can fulfil this description.
(2) Historical proof
The ancient Jewish historian Josephus
(first century A.D.) assures us that the
descendants of Magog (who was
Japheth's son and Noah's grandson)
migrated to an area north of Palestine.
But even prior to Josephus, the famous
Greek historian Herodotus (fifth
century B.C.) writes that Meshech's
descendants settled north of Palestine.
(3) Linguistic proof
Dr. John Walvoord writes concerning this,
"In Ezekiel 38, Gog is described as
'the prince of Rosh' (ASV). The
Authorized Version expresses it as the
'chief prince.' The translation
'the prince of Rosh' is a more literal
rendering of the Hebrew. 'Rosh' may be

the root of the modern term 'Russia.'
In the study of how ancient words come
into modern language, it is quite common
for the consonants to remain the same
and the vowels to be changed. In the
word 'Rosh,' if the vowel 'O' is
changed to 'U' it becomes the root
of the modern word 'Russia' with the
suffix added. In other words,
the word itself seems to be an early form
of the word from which the modern word
'Russia' comes. Genesius, the famous
lexicographer, gives the assurance that
this is a proper identification, that is,
that Rosh is an early form of the word
from which we get Russia. The two
terms 'Mesheck' and 'Tubal' also
correspond to some prominent words
in Russia. The term 'Mesheck' is similar
to the modern name 'Moscow' and 'Tubal'
is obviously similar to the name
of one of the prominent Asiatic provinces
of Russia, the province of Tobolsk.
When this evidence is put together,
it points to the conclusion that these
terms are early references to portions
of Russia; therefore the geographic
argument is reinforced by the linguistic
argument and supports the idea that
this invading force comes from Russia."[17]

b. The allies in the invasion

Ezekiel lists five nations who will join Russia

---

[17]John Walvoord, *The Nations in Prophecy* (Grand Rapids: Zondervan, 1967), pp. 107, 108. Used by permission.

during her invasion. These are Persia,
Ethiopia, Libya, Gomar, and Togarmah.
These may (although there is some
uncertainty) refer to the following present-day
nations:

> Persia — Modern Iran
> Ethiopia — Black African nations
> (South Africa)
> Libya — Arabic African nations
> (North Africa)
> Gomer — East Germany
> Togarmah — Southern Russia and the
> Cossacks, or perhaps Turkey

c. The reasons for the invasion

> (1) To cash in on the riches of Palestine
> (Ezek. 38:11, 12).
> (2) To control the Middle East
> Ancient conquerors have always known
> that he who would control Europe,
> Asia, and Africa must first control
> that Middle East bridge which leads
> to these three continents!
> (3) To challenge the authority of the
> antichrist (Dan. 11:40-44).

d. The chronology of the invasion

Here it is utterly impossible to be dogmatic.
The following is therefore only a suggested
possibility, based on Ezekiel 38 and
Daniel 11:40-44.

> (1) Following a preconceived plan,
> Egypt attacks Palestine from the south
> (Dan. 11:40a).
> (2) Russia thereupon invades Israel

from the north by both an amphibious
and a land attack (Dan. 11:40b).

(3) Russia does not stop in Israel,
but continues southward and double-
crosses her ally by occupying Egypt also
(Dan. 11:42, 43).

(4) While in Egypt, Russia hears
some disturbing news coming from
the East and North and hurriedly returns
to Palestine. We are not told what
the content of this news is. Several
theories have been offered:

> (a) That it contains the electrify-
> ing news that the antichrist
> has been assassinated, but has risen
> from the dead! See Revelation
> 13:3.

> (b) That it concerns itself with
> the impending counterattack of the
> Western leader (the antichrist).

> (c) That it warns of a con-
> frontation with China and India
> ("Kings of the East"), who may be
> mobilizing their troops.

e. The destruction of the invaders

Upon her return, Russia is soundly defeated
upon the mountains of Israel. This smashing
defeat is effected by the following events,
caused by God himself:

> (1) A mighty earthquake (Ezek.
> 38:19, 20).
> (2) Mutiny among the Russian troops
> (Ezek. 38:21).

(3) A plague among the troops
(Ezek. 38:22).
(4) Floods, great hailstones, fire
and brimstone (Ezek. 38:22; 39:6).

f. The results of the invasion

(1) Five-sixths (83%) of the Russian
soldiers are destroyed (Ezek. 39:2).

(2) The first grisly feast of God begins
(Ezek. 39:4, 17, 18, 19, 20).
A similar feast would seem to take place
later, after the battle of Armageddon
(Rev. 19:17, 18; Matt. 24:28).

(3) The Communistic threat will
cease forever.

(4) Seven months will be spent in
burying the dead (Ezek. 39:11-15).

(5) Seven years will be spent in burning
the weapons of war (Ezek. 39:9, 10).

Dr. John Walvoord writes the following
concerning this seven-year period:

"There are some . . . problems in the
passage which merit study. A reference
is made to bows and arrows,
to shields and chariots, and to swords.
These, of course, are antiquated weapons
from the standpoint of modern warfare.
The large use of horses is understandable,
as Russia today uses horses a great deal
in connection with their army. But why
should they use armor, spears,
bows and arrows? This certainly poses
a problem. There have been two or more

answers given. *One* of them is that
Ezekiel is using language with which
he was familiar — the weapons that were
common in his day — to anticipate
modern weapons. What he is saying
is that when this army comes, it will be
fully equipped with the weapons of war.
Such an interpretation, too, has problems.
We are told in the passage that they
used the wooden shafts of the spears
and the bow and arrows for kindling
wood. If these are symbols, it would be
difficult to burn symbols. However,
even in modern warfare there is a good
deal of wood used . . .

A second solution is that the battle
is preceded by a disarmament agreement
between nations. If this were the case,
it would be necessary to resort to
primitive weapons easily and secretly
made if a surprise attack were to be
achieved. This would allow a literal
interpretation of the passage.

A third solution has also been suggested
based on the premise that modern missile
warfare will have developed in that day
to a point where missiles will seek
out any considerable amount of metal.
Under these circumstances, it would be
necessary to abandon the large use
of metal weapons and substitute wood
such as is indicated in the primitive
weapons."[18]

---

[18]Walvoord, *The Nations in Prophecy*, pp. 115, 116.

2. The martyrdom of the two witnesses
(Rev. 11:7)

"And when they shall have finished their testimony,
the beast that ascendeth out of the bottomless
pit shall make war against them, and shall
overcome them, and kill them."

There is a hint in Revelation 11:8 that the
two witnesses will be crucified by the antichrist!

3. The martyrdom of the 144,000 Hebrew
evangelists (Rev. 14:1-5)

"And I looked, and lo, a Lamb stood on the
Mount Sion, and with him an hundred forty
and four thousand, having his Father's name written
in their foreheads" (Rev. 14:1).

4. The casting out of Heaven's monster
(Rev. 12:3-15)

   a. The identity of this monster

   There is no doubt whatever concerning
   the identity of this "creature from the clouds."
   He is pinned down by no less than four titles.

      (1) The Great Red Dragon — Rev.
      12:3
      (2) That Old Serpent — Rev. 12:9
      (3) The Devil — Rev. 12:9
      (4) Satan — Rev. 12:9

   b. The location of this monster

   Satan has been, is now, or shall be in one
   of the following locations:

      (1) In heaven, as God's anointed angel
      (past location — Ezek. 28:14)

(2) In heaven, as God's chief enemy
(present location — Job 1, 2)
(3) On earth, as the antichrist's
spiritual guide (future location,
during the tribulation — Rev. 12:12)
(4) In the bottomless pit (future,
during the millennium — Rev. 20:1-3)
(5) On earth again (future, after
the millennium — Rev. 20:8, 9)
(6) In the lake of fire (future
and forever — Rev. 20:10)

c. The activities of this monster

(1) He deceives all living unbelievers
(Rev. 12:9).
(2) He accuses all departed believers
(Rev. 12:10).
(3) He persecutes the nation Israel
(Rev. 12:13).

5. The destruction of the false church (Rev. 17:16)

"And the ten horns which thou sawest upon
the beast, these shall hate the whore, and shall make
her desolate and naked, and shall eat her flesh
and burn her with fire."

One of the most ironical turn of events in all history
will be the destruction of the false church.
For this evil organization will meet its doom
not at the hands of Gabriel, or the Father, or the Son,
or the Spirit, but the antichrist!

We have already seen how the false church
elevates the antichrist into power. But then
she apparently attempts to control him. He will have
none of it, however, and will destroy her buildings,
burn her holy books, and murder her priests!

The Last Half of the Tribulation (*3½ years*)

1. The full manifestation of the antichrist

After the judgment of Russia, the destruction
of the false church, and the murder of most
of God's preachers (the 144,000 and the two
witnesses), an unbelievable vacuum will un-
doubtedly settle down upon the world. The antichrist
will immediately exploit this. The following
is but a suggestion of the chronology of events
which may take place at this critical time.

a. The antichrist and his false prophet
make their headquarters in Jerusalem
after God destroys Russia.

b. Here in the holy city, perhaps during
a television speech, the antichrist is suddenly
assassinated, as millions of astonished viewers
watch (Rev. 13:3, 14).

c. Before his burial — perhaps during the
state funeral — he suddenly rises from
the dead. The world is electrified!

d. The antichrist is immediately worshiped
by the world as God.

e. The false prophet thereupon makes a statue
of the antichrist, causes it to speak,
and places it in the Holy of Holies
(Matt. 24:15; Dan. 9:27; 12:11; 2 Thess.
2:4).

f. A law is passed which stipulates that
no one can buy, sell, work, or obtain any

necessity of life unless he carries a special mark
on his right hand or his forehead
to identify him as a worshiper of the beast
(Rev. 13:16, 17).

g. The number of this mark is 666
(Rev. 13:18).

2. The worldwide persecution of Israel

"And at that time shall Michael stand up,
the great prince which standeth for the children
of thy people; and there shall be a time of trouble,
such as never was since there was a nation even
to that same time . . ." (Dan. 12:1).
"For, lo, I will raise up a shepherd in the land
which shall not visit those that be cut off,
neither shall seek the young one, nor heal that
that is broken, nor feed that that standeth still;
but he shall eat the flesh of the fat, and tear
their claws in pieces" (Zech. 11:16).
"For then shall be great tribulation, such as was not
since the beginning of the world to this time, no,
nor ever shall be" (Matt. 24:21).
"And when the dragon saw that he was cast unto
the earth, he persecuted the woman which brought
forth the manchild" (Rev. 12:13).
When the Israelites see the statue of the antichrist
standing in their Holy of Holies, the words of
Christ will come to their minds. He had warned
them of this very thing many centuries earlier
(Matt. 24:15-20).

At this point the Jews of the world will travel
down one of three roads:

a. Many Israelites will be killed by the
antichrist.

"And it shall come to pass that in all the land,
saith the Lord, two parts therein shall be
cut off and die; but the third shall be left
therein" (Zech. 13:8).

b.   Some Israelites will follow the antichrist.

"And then shall many be offended,
and shall betray one another, and shall hate
one another. And many false prophets shall
rise, and shall deceive many. And because
iniquity shall abound, the love of many
shall wax cold" (Matt. 24:10-12).
". . . I know the blasphemy of them
which say they are Jews, and are not,
but are the synagogue of Satan" (Rev. 2:9).
"Behold, I will make them of the synagogue
of Satan which say they are Jews,
and are not, but do lie; behold, I will make
them to come and worship before thy feet,
and to know that I have loved thee"
(Rev. 3:9).

c.   A remnant of Israel will be saved.

"And to the woman were given two wings
of a great eagle, that she might fly
into the wilderness, into her place, where
she is nourished for a time, and times,
and half a time, from the face of the serpent"
(Rev. 12:14).
"And I will bring the third part through the fire,
and will refine them as silver is refined,
and will try them as gold is tried; they shall
call on my name, and I will hear them:
I will say, It is my people; and they shall say,
The Lord is my God" (Zech. 13:9).

Thus it would seem that at least one-third
of Israel will remain true to God and be
allowed by him to escape into a special hiding
place for the duration of the Tribulation.
We shall now consider the location of this
hiding place. While it is not actually
specified in Scripture, many Bible students
believe that this place will be Petra.
This is based on the following three passages:

(1)   Zechariah 14:5
"And ye shall flee to the valley
of the mountains, for the valley of the
mountains shall reach unto Azal; yea,
ye shall flee . . . and the Lord my God
shall come, and all the saints with thee."
(The "Azal" mentioned here is thought
to be connected with Petra.)
(2)   Isaiah 63:1
"Who is this that cometh from Edom,
with dyed garments from Bozrah?"
The first few verses of Isaiah 63 deal
with the second coming of Christ.
He comes to Edom (of which Petra
is capital) and Bozrah (a city in Edom)
for some reason, and many believe that
reason is to receive his Hebrew remnant
who are hiding there.
(3)   Daniel 11:41
"He shall enter also into the glorious
land, and many countries shall be
overthrown; but these shall escape out
of his hand, even Edom. . . ."

Thus for some reason the land of Edom will
not be allowed to fall into the hands of the

antichrist. It is assumed by some that
the reason is to protect the remnant!

Many years ago the noted Bible scholar
W. E. Blackstone on the basis of these verses
hid thousands of copies of the New Testament
in and around the caves and rocks of Petra.
He felt that someday the terrified survivors of
the antichrist's bloodbath will welcome the
opportunity to read God's Word, preferring
it even over the Dow-Jones stock average
and the Wall Street Journal!

Petra has been called "the rainbow city,"
and once had 267,000 inhabitants. It was a
large market center at the junction of a
great caravan route. The city is inaccessible
except through the gorge or canyon in the
mountains, which is wide enough for only
two horses abreast. The perpendicular walls
of the gorge are from 400 to 700 feet high
and are brilliant in splendor, displaying
every color of the rainbow.

The old buildings, cut from the solid rock
of the mountain, still stand. A clear spring
bubbles over rose-red rocks. Wild figs grow on
the banks. Everything awaits Israel!

3. The Pouring out of the last seal judgment
(Rev. 8, 9; 11:15-19)

This final seal judgment consists of seven
trumpet plagues.

a. The sounding of the first trumpet

"The first angel sounded, and there followed
hail and fire mingled with blood,

and they were cast upon the earth;
and the third part of trees was burnt up,
and all green grass was burnt up"
(Rev. 8:7).

b. The sounding of the second trumpet

"And the second angel sounded, and as it were
a great mountain burning with fire was
cast into the sea; and the third part
of the sea became blood; and the third part
of the creatures which were in the sea,
and had life, died; and the third part
of the ships were destroyed" (Rev. 8:8, 9).

c. The sounding of the third trumpet

"And the third angel sounded, and there fell
a great star from heaven, burning as it were
a lamp, and it fell upon the third part
of the rivers, and upon the fountains of waters;
and the name of the star is called Wormwood;
and the third part of the waters became
wormwood; and many men died of the waters,
because they were made bitter"
(Rev. 8:10, 11).

This star could refer to a meteor containing
stifling and bitter gases which fall on the Alps
or some other freshwater source.

d. The sounding of the fourth trumpet

"And the fourth angel sounded, and the third
part of the sun was smitten, and the third
part of the moon, and the third part
of the stars; so as the third part of them
was darkened, and the day shone not

for a third part of it, and the night likewise"
(Rev. 8:12).

Our Lord may have had this trumpet judgment
in mind when he spoke the following words:

"And except those days should be shortened,
there should no flesh be saved; but for
the elect's sake those days shall be shortened"
(Matt. 24:22).
"And there shall be signs in the sun,
and in the moon, and in the stars . . ."
(Luke 21:25).

The Old Testament prophecy of Amos
is also significant here:

"And it shall come to pass in that day,
saith the Lord God, that I will cause the sun
to go down at noon, and I will darken the earth
in the clear day" (Amos 8:9).

e. The sounding of the fifth trumpet

"And the fifth angel sounded, and I saw a star
fall from heaven unto the earth; and to him
was given the key of the bottomless pit"
(Rev. 9:1).

> (1) This pit is opened and hellish,
> locust-like demons come out.
> (2) For five months these fowl
> creatures torture unsaved mankind with
> agonizing stings from their tails.

f. The sounding of the sixth trumpet

"And the sixth angel sounded . . ."
(Rev. 9:13).

(1)   Four imprisoned demons are
released from the river Euphrates.
(2)   They lead an army of horsemen-like
demons numbering 200 million.
By normal standards this mighty cavalry
would occupy a territory one mile wide
and eighty-seven miles long!
(3) They will kill one-third of mankind
by fire and smoke.

Dr. W. A. Criswell writes the following words:

"The voice cries, 'Loose the four angels which
are bound over the great river Euphrates.'
The River Euphrates begins in the Armenian
Mountains, some of the highest in the earth.
Flooded in the springtime with melting
snows, it goes through the Taurus Range
and through the Mesopotamian Valley
down to the Persian Gulf. The Euphrates
River, the most important, the longest, the
biggest in all Western Asia, was the place
where sin was first known, where misery first
began, where the first lie was told, where the
first murder was committed, where the
first grave was dug. The Euphrates River
was the scene of the two great apostasies
before and after the flood. The Euphrates
River was the scene of the rise of Israel's
greatest and most oppressive enemies.
The Euphrates River was the scene of the
long years in which the children of Israel
dragged out the wearisome days of their
captivity. The Euphrates River was the scene
of the rise of those great world empires
that oppressed civilization in the ancient day
— cruel empires like Assyria, like Babylon,

like the Persians and the Medes. There in
that place these four angels, these magnates
of evil, are chained. They have in their hands
power of awful destruction and satanic evil.
They are prepared for an hour, and a day,
and a month, and a year. At the exact
second, at the exact moment in God's calendar,
their vile judgment is loosed upon this
world."[19]

g. The sounding of the seventh trumpet

"And the seventh angel sounded; and
there were great voices in heaven, saying,
The kingdoms of this world are become
the kingdoms of our Lord, and of his Christ;
and he shall reign for ever and ever"
(Rev. 11:15).

This seventh angel proclaims the glorious news
that very soon now the Lord Jesus Christ
will take over the nations of this world
as their rightful ruler. The announcement
produces a twofold reaction:

(1) The citizens of heaven rejoice;

(2) The nations of the earth become
angry.

The seventh angel prepares us not only for
the consummation of the ages, but also
for the explanation for all things.

"But in the days of the voice of the seventh
angel, when he shall begin to sound, the
mystery of God should be finished . . ."
(Rev. 10:7).

---

[19]W. A. Criswell, *Expository Sermons on Revelation* (Grand Rapids: Zondervan, 1961-66), p. 190. Used by permission.

Dr. W. A. Criswell writes again,

"The mystery of God is the long delay of our
Lord in taking the kingdom unto Himself
and in establishing righteousness in the earth.
The mystery of God is seen in these thousands
of years in which sin and death run riot. There
is no village and there is no hamlet without
its raging, and there is no human heart without
its dark, black drop. There is no life without
its tears and its sorrows. There is no home
that ultimately does not break up, and there
is no family that does not see the circle
of the home dissolve in the depths of the grave.
There is no life that does not end in death.
The pages of history, from the time of the
first murder until this present hour, are written
in blood, tears and death. The mystery is
the delay of God in taking the kingdom unto
Himself. That is the most inexplicable
mystery that mind could dream of,
the mystery of the presence of evil. For these
thousands of years, God has allowed Satan
to wrap his vicious, slimy, filthy, cruel
tentacles around human life and around
this earth. Does God know it? Is He
indifferent to it? Is He not able to cope with
it? Oh, the mystery of the delay of God!
That mystery has brought more stumbling to
the faith of God's people than any other
experience in all life. The infidel, the atheist,
the agnostic and the unbeliever laugh and
mock us, and God lets them mock and laugh.
The enemies of righteousness and the
enemies of all that we hold dear rise and
increase in power and spread blood and

darkness over the face of the earth, and
we wonder where God is. Our missionaries
are slain, our churches are burned to the
ground, people in this earth by uncounted
millions and millions are oppressed,
living in despair, and God just looks. He
seemingly does not intervene; He does not say
anything, and He does not move. Sin just
develops. It goes on and on. Oh, the mystery
of the delay of the Lord God! But
somewhere beyond the starry sky there stands
a herald angel with a trumpet in his hand,
and by the decree of the Lord God Almighty,
there is a day, there is an hour, there is a
moment, there is an elected time when the
angel shall sound and the kingdoms of this
world shall become the kingdoms of our God
and of His Christ."[20]

4. The messages of three special angels
(Rev. 14:6-12)

a. The first message

"And I saw another angel fly in the midst
of heaven, having the everlasting gospel
to preach unto them that dwell on the earth,
and to every nation, and kindred,
and tongue, and people, saying with a loud
voice, Fear God, and give glory to him;
for the hour of his judgment is come;
and worship him that made heaven, and earth,
and the sea, and the fountains of waters"
(Rev. 14:6, 7).

---

[20]Criswell, *Sermons on Revelation*, pp. 199, 200.

We see in this verse something absolutely
unique — an angel of God preaching the
gospel to sinners! Up to this point
God has used only *men* to reach other men
(see Acts 1:8; 2 Peter 1:21; 2 Cor. 4:7).
But now, due to the severity of the
Tribulation, angels will be used! Thus, God,
like Paul, becomes all things to all men,
that by all means he might save some
(1 Cor. 9:22)!

b. The second message

"And there followed another angel, saying,
Babylon is fallen, is fallen, that great city,
because she made all nations drink of the wine
of the wrath of her fornication" (Rev. 14:8).

This second message is to announce
the imminent destruction of political
and economic Babylon (see Rev. 18).

c. The third message

"And the third angel followed them,
saying with a loud voice, If any man worship
the beast and his image, and receive
his mark in his forehead, or in his hand,
the same shall drink of the wine of the wrath
of God, which is poured out without mixture
into the cup of his indignation;
and he shall be tormented with fire and
brimstone in the presence of the holy angels
and in the presence of the Lamb;
and the smoke of their torment ascendeth
up forever and ever; and they have no rest
day nor night, who worship the beast

and his image, and whosoever receiveth
the mark of his name" (Rev. 14:9-11).

Here is the last hellfire-and-brimstone message
that will ever be preached to the unsaved,
and it is delivered not by a Jonathan Edwards
or a Billy Sunday, but by an angel!
But apparently no one responds to the
invitation.

5. The pouring out of the seven bowls ("vials")
of judgment (Rev. 16)

"And I heard a great voice out of the temple
saying to the seven angels, Go your ways,
and pour out the vials of the wrath of God
upon the earth" (Rev. 16:1).

a. The first vial judgment

"And the first went, and poured out his vial
upon the earth; and there fell a noisome
and grievous sore upon the men which
had the mark of the beast, and upon them
which worshipped his image" (Rev. 16:2).

J. Vernon McGee writes,

"God is engaged in germ warfare upon
the followers of antichrist . . . These putrefying
sores are worse than leprosy or cancer.
This compares to the sixth plague in Egypt,
and is the same type of sore or boil
(see Exod. 9:8-12)."[21]

b. The second vial judgment

"And the second angel poured out his vial
upon the sea; and it became as the blood

---

[21]McGee, *Reveling through Revelation*, p. 36.

of a dead man; and every living soul
died in the sea" (Rev. 16:3).

Dr. Charles Ryrie writes the following
concerning this plague:

"The second bowl is poured on the sea,
with the result that the waters become blood
and every living thing in the sea dies.
The 'as' is misplaced in the Authorized
Version, the correct reading being
'became blood as of a dead man.' The vivid
image is of a dead person wallowing
in his own blood. The seas will wallow
in blood. Under the second trumpet,
one-third of the sea creatures died (8:9);
now the destruction is complete.
The stench and disease that this will cause
along the shores of the seas of the earth
are unimaginable."[22]

c. The third vial judgment

"And the third angel poured out his vial
upon the rivers and fountains of waters;
and they became blood. And I heard the angel
of the waters say, Thou art righteous, O Lord,
which art and wast and shalt be,
because thou hast judged thus. For they
have shed the blood of saints and prophets,
and thou hast given them blood to drink;
for they are worthy. And I heard
another out of the altar say, Even so,
Lord God Almighty, true and righteous
are thy judgments" (Rev. 16:4-7).

[22]Ryrie, *Revelation,* p. 97.

Two significant things may be noted
in these verses:

> (1) This third vial judgment is,
> among other things, an answer to the cry
> of the martyrs under the altar at the
> beginning of the Tribulation. Their
> prayer at that time was, "How long,
> O Lord, holy and true, dost thou not
> judge and avenge our blood on them
> that dwell on the earth?" (Rev. 6:10).
> (2) These verses indicate that God
> has assigned a special angel as
> superintendent of earth's waterworks.
> When we compare this with Revelation
> 7:1, where we are told that four other
> angels control the world's winds,
> we realize that even during the
> hellishness of the Tribulation this world
> is still controlled by God!

d. The fourth vial judgment

"And the fourth angel poured out his vial
upon the sun; and power was given unto him
to scorch men with fire. And men were
scorched with great heat, and blasphemed
the name of God, which hath power over
these plagues; and they repented not to give
him glory" (Rev. 16:8, 9).

Perhaps the two most illuminating passages
in Scripture about man's total depravity
can be found in Revelation 9:20, 21 and
Revelation 16:9. Both sections deal
with the world's attitude toward God
during the Tribulation.

> (1) "And the rest of the men which
> were not killed by these plagues yet
> repented not of the works of their hands.
> that they should not worship devils,
> and idols of gold, and silver, and brass,
> and stone, and of wood, which neither
> can see, nor hear, nor walk; neither
> repented they of their murders, nor of
> their sorceries, nor of their fornication,
> nor of their thefts" (Rev. 9:20, 21).
> (2) ". . . and they repented not
> to give him glory" (Rev. 16:9).

What do these verses prove? They prove that
in spite of horrible wars, of terrible famines,
of darkened skies, of raging fires, of bloody
seas, of stinging locusts, of demonic
persecutions, of mighty earthquakes, of
falling stars, and of cancerous sores, sinful
mankind *still will not repent!*

e. The fifth vial judgment

"And the fifth angel poured out his vial
upon the seat of the beast; and his kingdom
was full of darkness; and they gnawed
their tongues for pain, and blasphemed
the God of heaven because of their pains
and their sores, and repented not of their
deeds" (Rev. 16:10, 11).

This plague, poured out upon "the seat
of the beast" (literally his "throne"),
will apparently concentrate itself upon
the ten nations of the revived Roman Empire.
Again we read those tragic words, "and
repented not of their deeds."

f. The sixth vial judgment

"And the sixth angel poured out his vial
upon the great river Euphrates; and the water
thereof was dried up, that the way
of the kings of the east might be prepared.
And I saw three unclean spirits like frogs
come out of the mouth of the dragon,
and out of the mouth of the beast, and out
of the mouth of the false prophet. For they
are the spirits of devils, working miracles,
which go forth unto the kings of the earth
and of the whole world, to gather them to
the battle of that great day of God
Almighty" (Rev. 16:12-14).

Here the God of heaven employs psychological
warfare upon his enemies, conditioning them
to gather themselves together in the near
future at Armageddon.

g. The seventh vial judgment

"And the seventh angel poured out his vial
into the air; and there came a great voice out
of the temple of heaven, from the throne,
saying, It is done. And there were voices,
and thunders, and lightnings; and there
was a great earthquake, such as was not
since men were upon the earth, so mighty an
earthquake, and so great. And the great city
was divided into three parts, and the cities
of the nations fell; and great Babylon
came in remembrance before God, to give
unto her the cup of the wine of the fierceness
of his wrath. And every island fled away,
and the mountains were not found.

And there fell upon men a great hail out
of heaven, every stone about the weight
of a talent; and men blasphemed God
because of the plague of the hail,
for the plague thereof was exceeding great"
(Rev. 16:17-21).

Thus ends the seal, trumpet, and vial judgments. Three items in this last vial
are worthy of observation:

(1) The statement "It is done" is the
second of three biblical occurrences
in which this phrase is connected
with some great event. The first event
was Calvary and the last will be
the threshold of eternity.

"When Jesus therefore had received
the vinegar, he said, It is finished;
and he bowed his head, and gave up
the ghost" (John 19:30).
"And he said unto me, It is done.
I am Alpha and Omega, the beginning
and the end. I will give unto him
that is athirst of the fountain of the water
of life freely" (Rev. 21:6).

(2) The world's greatest earthquake
takes place

The intensity of an earthquake is
measured on an instrument called a
Richter scale. The greatest magnitude
ever recorded so far has been 8.9.
The greatest loss of life due to an earthquake occurred on January 23, 1556,
in Shensi Province, China, and killed
some 830,000 people.

However, that earthquake will be
but a mild tremor compared to the
tribulational earthquake, which, we are
told, will level all the great cities
of the world!

(3) The world's greatest shower of
hailstones comes crashing down on
mankind. These gigantic icy chunks
will weigh up to 125 pounds apiece!

6. The Sudden Destruction of Economic and Political Babylon (Rev. 18)

"And there followed another angel, saying,
Babylon is fallen, is fallen, that great city,
because she made all nations drink of the wine
of the wrath of her fornication" (Rev. 14:8).
". . . and great Babylon came in remembrance
before God, to give unto her the cup of the wine
of the fierceness of his wrath" (Rev. 16:19).
"And after these things I saw another angel
come down from heaven, having great power;
and the earth was lightened with his glory. And he
cried mightily with a strong voice, saying, Babylon
the great is fallen, is fallen . . ." (Rev. 18:1, 2).

It is the opinion of this study that literal Babylon
will be rebuilt during the Tribulation. The Old
Testament city of Babylon is mentioned more times
in the Bible than any other city with the exception
of Jerusalem. It is mentioned no less than
260 times!

What will this restored "City of Satan" be like?
Dr. Lehman Strauss has given us an excellent
description of ancient Babylon.

"Babylon was founded by Nimrod, the great-

grandson of Noah (Gen. 10:8-10). Surviving
a series of conflicts, it became one of the most
magnificent and luxurious cities in the known world.
Superbly constructed, it spread over an area
of fifteen square miles, the Euphrates River
flowing diagonally across the city. The famous
historian Herodotus said the city was surrounded
by a wall 350 feet high and 87 feet thick —
wide enough for six chariots to drive abreast.
Around the top of the wall were 250 watchtowers
placed in strategic locations. Outside the huge wall
was a large ditch, or moat, which surrounded
the city and was kept filled with water
from the Euphrates River. The large ditch
was meant to serve as an additional protection
against attacking enemies, for any attacking enemy
would have to cross this body of water first
before approaching the great wall. The cost
of constructing this military defense was estimated
to be in excess of one billion dollars. When we
consider the value of a billion dollars in those
days, plus the fact that it was all built with slave
labor, one can imagine something of the wonder
and magnificence of this famous city.

"But in addition to being a bastion for protection,
Babylon was a place of beauty. The famous
hanging gardens of Babylon are on record yet
today as one of the seven wonders of the world.
Arranged in an area 400 feet square, and raised
in perfectly-cut terraces one above the other,
they soared to a height of 350 feet. Viewers
could make their way to the top by means of
stairways, which were 10 feet wide. Each terrace
was covered with a large stone slab topped
with a thick layer of asphalt, two courses of brick

cemented together, and, finally, plates of lead
to prevent any leakage of water. On top of all this
was an abundance of rich, fertile earth planted
with vines, flowers, shrubs, and trees.
From a distance these hanging gardens gave
the appearance of a beautiful mountainside,
when viewed from the level plains of the valley.
The estimated cost to build this thing of beauty
ran into hundreds of millions of dollars.

"The tower of Babel with its temples of worship
presented an imposing sight. The tower itself
sat on a base 300 feet in breadth and rose to a height
of 300 feet. The one chapel on the top
contained an image alone reported to be worth
$17,500,000, and sacred vessels, used in worshipping
Babylonian gods, estimated at a value of
$200,000,000. In addition to this wealth
and grandeur the temple contained the most
elaborate and expensive furniture ever to adorn
any place of worship."[23]

This, then, is what ancient Babylon looked like.
And who can doubt that the revived Babylon
will far outshine the glories of the old? As Dr.
J. Vernon McGee suggests,

"In this day Babylon will dominate and rule
the world; she will have the first total dictatorship.
The stock market will be read from Babylon;
Babylon will set the styles for the world; a play
to be successful will have to be a success in Babylon.
And everything in the city is in rebellion against
Almighty God and centers in Antichrist. No one
dreamed that this great city would be judged.

---

[23]Lehman Strauss, *The Prophecies of Daniel* (Neptune, N. J.: Loizeaux, 1969), pp. 147, 148. Used by permission.

Yet by the time the sun went down, Babylon
was nothing but smoldering ruins. When the news
goes out the world is stunned, and then begins
the wail. The whole world will howl when Babylon
goes down. You will have to tune down
your earphones if you are on the moon."[24]

We shall now note several features involved in the
destruction of Babylon.

    a. The source of her destruction — God
himself! See Revelation 18:8, 20.

    b. The means of her destruction — it would
almost seem that atomic power of some sort
is used to accomplish this! This is strongly
suggested by the swiftness of the judgment,
the raging fires, and the distance kept
by those who watched her burn — possibly
due to fear of radioactive fallout!
See Revelation 18:9, 10, 15, 17, 18, 19.

    c. The reaction to her destruction

        (1) By those on earth
        "And they cast dust on their heads, and
cried, weeping and wailing, saying,
Alas, alas, that great city, wherein
were made rich all that had ships in the
sea by reason of her costliness!
For in one hour is she made desolate"
(Rev. 18:19).

        (2) By those in heaven
        "Rejoice over her, thou heaven,
and ye holy apostles and prophets;

---

[24]McGee, *Reveling through Revelation*, p. 6.

for God hath avenged you on her"
(Rev. 18:20).

There are three events in the Tribulation
which cause all of heaven to rejoice.

(a) When Satan is cast out
(Rev. 12:12).

(b) When Babylon is destroyed
(Rev. 18:20).

(c) When the Lamb is married
to the church (Rev. 19:7).

d. The reasons for her destruction

(1) Because the city will become
the headquarters of all demonic activity
during the Tribulation (Rev. 18:2).

(2) Because of her devilish pride
(Rev. 18:7).

(3) Because of her gross materialism.
This wicked city will import and export
twenty-eight principal items of
merchandise, beginning with gold
and ending with the bodies of men
(Rev. 18:12, 13)!

(4) Because of her drug activities
(Rev. 18:23).

(5) Because of her bloodshedding
(Rev. 18:24).

e. The Old Testament foreshadows
of her destruction

On the night of October 13, 539 B.C.,
the Babylon of the Old Testament was
captured by the Medes and Persians.
Just prior to this, Daniel the prophet had read
the fearful words of God to a frightened

Belshazzar: ". . . God hath numbered
thy kingdom, and finished it. . . . Thou art
weighed in the balances, and art found
wanting. . . . Thy kingdom is divided . . ."
(Dan. 5:26-28).

Someday God himself will once again write
these fearsome words across the skies
of Babylon!

7. The Battle of Armageddon (Rev. 16:16)

The Holy Spirit of God has chosen five capable
authors to describe for us in clear and chilling
language that most famous of all battles —
Armageddon! These five authors include David,
Isaiah, Joel, Zechariah, and John.

"Why do the nations rage, and the peoples imagine
a vain thing? The kings of the earth set themselves,
and the rulers take counsel together against
the Lord and against his anointed, saying, Let us
break their bands asunder, and cast away
their cords from us. He who sitteth in the heavens
shall laugh; the Lord shall have them in derision.
Then shall he speak unto them in his wrath,
and vex them in his great displeasure. Thou shalt
break them with a rod of iron; thou shalt dash them
in pieces like a potter's vessel" (Psa. 2:1-5, 9).

"Come near, ye nations, to hear; and hearken,
ye peoples; let the earth hear, and all that is therein;
the world, and all things that come forth from it.
For the indignation of the Lord is upon all nations,
and his fury upon all their armies; he hath
utterly destroyed them, he hath delivered them
to the slaughter. Their slain also shall be cast out,
and their stench shall come up out of their carcasses,

and the mountains shall be melted with their blood.
And all the host of heaven shall be dissolved,
and the heavens shall be rolled together as a scroll;
and all their host shall fall down, as the leaf
falleth off from the vine, and as a falling fig
from the fig tree. For my sword shall be bathed
in heaven; behold, it shall come down upon Edom,
and upon the people of my curse, to judgment.
The sword of the Lord is filled with blood;
it is made fat with fatness, and with the blood
of lambs and goats, with the fat of the kidneys
of rams; for the Lord hath a sacrifice in Bozrah,
and a great slaughter in the land of Edom"
(Isa. 34:1-6).

"I have trodden the winepress alone, and of the
peoples there was none with me; for I will tread
them in mine anger, and trample them in my fury;
and their blood shall be sprinkled upon my
garments, and I will stain all my raiment. For the
day of vengeance is in mine heart, and the year
of my redeemed is come. And I will tread down
the peoples in mine anger, and make them drunk
in my fury, and I will bring down their strength
to the earth" (Isa. 63:3, 4, 6).

"I will also gather all nations, and will bring them
down into the Valley of Jehoshaphat, and will judge
them there for my people and for my heritage,
Israel, whom they have scattered among the nations,
and parted my land. . . . Proclaim this among
the Gentiles, Prepare war, wake up the mighty men,
let all the men of war draw near; let them come up;
beat your plowshares into swords, and your
pruninghooks into spears; let the weak say,
I am strong. Assemble yourselves, and come,
all ye nations, and gather yourselves together

round about; there cause thy mighty ones
to come down, O Lord. Let the nations be wakened,
and come up to the Valley of Jehoshaphat;
for there will I sit to judge all the nations round about.
Put in the sickle; for the harvest is ripe; come,
get you down; for the press is full, the vats
overflow; for their wickedness is great.
Multitudes, multitudes in the valley of decision;
for the day of the Lord is near in the valley
of decision. The sun and the moon shall be
darkened, and the stars shall withdraw their shining.
The Lord also shall roar out of Zion, and utter
his voice from Jerusalem, and the heavens
and the earth shall shake; but the Lord will be
the hope of his people, and the strength of the
children of Israel" (Joel 3:2, 9-16).

"Behold, I will make Jerusalem a cup of trembling
unto all the peoples round about, when they shall be
in the siege both against Judah and against
Jerusalem" (Zech. 12:2).

"For I will gather all nations against Jerusalem
to battle; and the city shall be taken, and the houses
rifled, and the women ravished; and half of the city
shall go forth into captivity, and the residue
of the people shall not be cut off from the city.
Then shall the Lord go forth, and fight against
those nations, as when he fought in the day
of battle. . . . And this shall be the plague
with which the Lord will smite all the peoples
that have fought against Jerusalem: their flesh
shall consume away while they stand upon their feet,
and their eyes shall consume away in their holes,
and their tongue shall consume away in their
mouth" (Zech. 14:2, 3, 12).

"And I looked, and behold, a white cloud,
and upon the cloud one sat like the Son of man,
having on his head a golden crown, and in his hand
a sharp sickle. And another angel came out
of the temple, crying with a loud voice to him
that sat on the cloud, Thrust in thy sickle, and reap;
for the time is come for thee to reap; for the harvest
of the earth is ripe. And he that sat on the cloud
thrust in his sickle on the earth, and the earth
was reaped. And another angel came out of the
temple which is in heaven, he also having
a sharp sickle. And another angel came out from
the altar, which had power over fire, and cried
with a loud cry to him that had the sharp sickle,
saying, Thrust in thy sharp sickle, and gather
the clusters of the vine of the earth, for her grapes
are fully ripe. And the angel thrust his sickle
into the earth, and gathered the vine of the earth,
and cast it into the great winepress of the wrath
of God. And the winepress was trodden
without the city, and blood came out of the
winepress, even unto the horse bridles, by the space
of a thousand and six hundred furlongs"
(Rev. 14:14-20).

"And he gathered them together into a place called
in the Hebrew tongue Armageddon" (Rev. 16:16).

"And I saw heaven opened, and behold,
a white horse; and he that sat upon him was called
Faithful and True, and in righteousness he doth
judge and make war. His eyes were as a flame
of fire, and on his head were many crowns;
and he had a name written that no man knew
but he himself. And he was clothed with a vesture
dipped in blood; and his name is called
The Word of God.

"And the armies which were in heaven followed
him upon white horses, clothed in fine linen,
white and clean.

"And out of his mouth goeth a sharp sword,
that with it he should smite the nations; and he
shall rule them with a rod of iron; and he treadeth
the winepress of the fierceness and wrath of
Almighty God. And he hath on his vesture
and on his thigh a name written, KING OF KINGS
AND LORD OF LORDS.

"And I saw an angel standing in the sun; and he
cried with a loud voice, saying to all the fowls
that fly in the midst of heaven, Come and gather
yourselves together unto the supper of the great God,
that ye may eat the flesh of kings, and the flesh
of captains, and the flesh of mighty men, and the
flesh of horses and of them that sit on them,
and the flesh of all men, both free and bond,
both small and great.

"And I saw the beast, and the kings of the earth,
and their armies, gathered together to make war
against him that sat on the horse, and against
his army. And the beast was taken, and with him
the false prophet that wrought miracles before him,
with which he deceived them that had received
the mark of the beast, and them that worshipped
his image. These both were cast alive
into a lake of fire burning with brimstone.

"And the remnant were slain with the sword
of him that sat upon the horse, which sword
proceeded out of his mouth; and all the fowls
were filled with their flesh" (Rev. 19:11-21).

In his little booklet entitled *Profiles of Prophecy,*
Dr. S. Franklin Logsdon writes,

"A former president of the Norwegian Academy
of Sciences, helped by historians from Britain,
Egypt, Germany and India, and using an electronic
computer, has found that since 3600 B.C. the world
has known only 292 years of peace. In this period
of more than 55 centuries there have been
14,531 wars, large and small, in which more than
3.6 billion people were killed. Since 650 B.C.,
there have been 1,656 arms races, all except
16 ending in war, and those 16 ended in
economic collapse for the countries concerned."[25]

But this coming War of Armageddon will be
by far the biggest, boldest, bloodiest, most brazen,
and most blasphemous of all times! We shall now
consider the negative and positive elements
of this war.

Negative

a. Armageddon is not the same as the
Russian invasion of Ezekiel 38. Note
the differences:

(1) Russia invades from the north,
but at Armageddon the nations come
from all directions.
(2) Russia invades to capture Israel's
wealth, but this invasion is to destroy
the Lamb and his people.
(3) Gog leads the Russian invasion,
but the antichrist leads this one.

b. Armageddon is not the final war
in the Bible — the final war occurs after the

---

[25]S. Franklin Logsdon, *Profiles in Prophecy* (Grand Rapids: Zondervan, 1969), p. 54. Used by permission.

millennium (Rev. 20:7-9). Armageddon
takes place at'the end of the Tribulation.

Positive

a. The location of the battle

Dr. Herman A. Hoyt aptly describes the
location:

"The staggering dimensions of this conflict
can scarcely be conceived by man.
The battlefield will stretch from Megiddo
on the north (Zech. 12:11; Rev. 16:16)
to Edom on the south (Isa. 34:5, 6; 63:1),
a distance of sixteen hundred furlongs —
approximately two hundred miles. It will
reach from the Mediterranean Sea on the west
to the hills of Moab on the east,
a distance of almost one hundred miles.
It will include the Valley of Jehoshaphat
(Joel 3:2, 12) and the Plains of Esdraelon.
At the center of the entire area will be the city
of Jerusalem (Zech. 14:1, 2). Into this area
the multiplied millions of men, doubtless
approaching 400 million, will be crowded
for the final holocaust of humanity.
The kings with their armies will come from
the north and the south, from the east
and from the west. . . . In the most dramatic
sense this will be the 'Valley of decision'
for humanity (Joel 3:14) and the great
winepress into which will be poured
the fierceness of the wrath of Almighty God
(Rev. 19:15)."[26]

---

[26]Herman A. Hoyt, *The End Time* (Chicago: Moody, 1969), p. 163. Used
by permission.

Thus there would seem to be at least
four important names involved in the battle
of Armageddon:

> (1) The Valley of Jehoshaphat — a
> valley situated just east of Jerusalem,
> between the Holy City and the Mount
> of Olives. See Joel 3:2, 12.
> (2) The Valley of Esdraelon —
> a valley twenty miles long and fourteen
> miles wide, situated north and west of
> Jerusalem between the Holy City
> and the Mediterranean Sea.
> (3) Megiddo — a flat plain located
> in the Valley of Esdraelon (Zech. 12:11).
> (4) Bozrah — a city in Edom,
> east of the Jordan River and near Petra,
> the capital of Edom. These two cities
> will play an important role during
> the second coming of our Lord.
> See Isaiah 34:6 and 63:1.

Marvin Vincent writes concerning Armageddon
and its location,

"Megiddo was in the plain of Esdraelon,
which has been a chosen place for encamp-
ment in every contest carried on in Palestine
from the days of . . . Assyria unto the
disastrous march of Napoleon Bonaparte from
Egypt into Syria. Jews, Gentiles, Saracens,
Christian Crusaders, and anti-Christian
Frenchmen; Egyptians, Persians, Druses,
Turks, and Arabs, warriors of every nation
that is under heaven, have pitched their tents
on the plains of Esdraelon, and have

beheld the banners of their nation wet with the dews of Mt. Tabor and Mt. Hermon."[27]

In addition to church history, a number of battles took place in this area, as reported by the Old Testament:

(1) It was here that Deborah and Barak defeated the Canaanites (Judges 4, 5).
(2) It was here that Gideon defeated the Midianites (Judges 7).
(3) It was here that the Philistines defeated and killed Saul (1 Sam. 31).
(4) It was here that David defeated Goliath (1 Sam. 17).
(5) It was here that an Egyptian king killed Josiah (2 Kings 23).

b. The reasons for the battle

What will draw all the nations of the world into the area of Armageddon? They will gather themselves there for perhaps various reasons. It would seem that the following are three of the more important reasons:

(1) Because of the sovereignty of God. In at least five distinct passages we are told that God himself will gather the nations here:
". . . he hath delivered them to the slaughter" (Isa. 34:2).
"I will also gather all nations, and will bring them down into the valley of Jehoshaphat . . ." (Joel 3:2).

[27]Marvin Vincent, *Word Studies in the New Testament* (Grand Rapids: Eerdman, 1957), pp. 542, 543. Quoted by Pentecost, *Things to Come*, p. 341.

"For I will gather all nations against
Jerusalem to battle . . ." (Zech. 14:2).
". . . For my determination is to gather
the nations. . . . to pour upon them
mine indignation, even all my
fierce anger . . ." (Zeph. 3:8).
"And he gathered them together into
a place called in the Hebrew tongue
Armageddon" (Rev. 16:16).
(2) Because of the deception of Satan
(Rev. 16:13, 14).
In this passage we are told that three
special unclean spirits will trick the
nations into gathering at Armageddon.
(3) Because of the hatred of the nations
for Christ.

> (a) A number of passages tell us
> of this devilish hatred (Psa. 2:1-3;
> Rev. 11:18).
> (b) The nations, led by the
> antichrist, will doubtless realize the
> imminent return of Christ
> (Rev. 11:15; 12:12).
> (c) They will also be aware of
> his touching down on the Mount
> of Olives (Zech. 14:4; Acts
> 1:9-12).
> (d) Thus it is not unreasonable
> to assume they will gather in that
> area to destroy him at the moment
> of his return to earth!

c. The chronology of the battle

> (1) The drying up of the Euphrates
> River (Rev. 16:12)

Dr. Donald Barnhouse quotes Seiss in describing this:

"From time immemorial the Euphrates with its tributaries has been a great and formidable boundary between the peoples east of it and those west of it. It runs a distance of 1800 miles, and is scarcely fordable anywhere or at any time. It is from three to twelve hundred yards wide, and from ten to thirty feet in depth; and most of the time it is still deeper and wider. It was the boundary of the dominion of Solomon, and is repeatedly spoken of as the northeast limit of the lands promised to Israel. . . . History frequently refers to the great hindrance the Euphrates has been to military movements; and it has always been a line of separation between the peoples living east of it and those living west of it."[28]

Thus, when this watery barrier is removed tens of millions of soldiers from China, India, and other Asian powers will march straight for Armageddon and destruction!

(2) The destruction of Jerusalem
Perhaps the saddest event during the Tribulation will be the siege and destruction of the Holy City. This will be the 47th and last take-over

[28]Barnhouse, *Revelation*, p. 301.

of the beloved city of David. The
following passages bear this out:

"Behold, I will make Jerusalem a cup
of trembling unto all the people round
about, when they shall be in the siege . . ."
(Zech. 12:2).
"For I will gather all nations against
Jerusalem to battle; and the city shall be
taken, and the houses rifled, and the
women ravished; and half the city
shall go forth into captivity . . ."
(Zech. 14:2).
"And when ye shall see Jerusalem
compassed with armies, then know that
the desolation thereof is nigh"
(Luke 21:20).

When these two events transpire,
both the angels in paradise and the
demons in perdition will surely hold their
breath. The reason for their suspense
will be discussed in the next major section.

VI. THE SECOND COMING OF CHRIST

The greatest day in history did not take place on July 20, 1969, when Astronaut Neil Armstrong walked on the moon, as President Richard Nixon said. Up till that time, the greatest day had occurred during an April Sunday morning some 2000 years ago, when the crucified Savior rose again from the dead! But God is preparing an even greater, grander, and more glorious day than the resurrection of his beloved Son — and that event is his return to earth again! Surely John the Apostle must have penned the following words with grape-sized goose pimples!

"And the seventh angel sounded; and there were great voices in heaven, saying, The kingdoms of this world are become the kingdoms of our Lord, and of his Christ; and he shall reign forever and ever" (Rev. 11:15).

"And I saw heaven opened, and behold, a white horse; and he that sat upon him was called Faithful and True, and in righteousness he doth judge and make war. His eyes were as a flame of fire, and on his head were many crowns; and he had a name written that no man knew but he himself. And he was clothed with a vesture dipped in blood; and his name is called The Word of God. And the armies which were in heaven followed him upon white horses, clothed in fine linen, white and clean. And out of his mouth goeth a sharp sword, that with it he should smite the nations; and he shall rule them with a rod of iron; and he treadeth the winepress of the fierceness and wrath of Almighty God. And he hath on his vesture

and on his thigh a name written, KING OF KINGS
AND LORD OF LORDS" (Rev. 19:11-16).

A. The Chronology of the Second Coming of Christ

1. It begins with fearful manifestations in the skies.

"Immediately after the tribulation of those days
shall the sun be darkened, and the moon shall not
give her light, and the stars shall fall from heaven,
and the powers of the heavens shall be shaken"
(Matt. 24:29).
"And there shall be signs in the sun, and in
the moon, and in the stars; and upon the earth
distress of nations, with perplexity, the sea
and the waves roaring, men's hearts failing them
for fear . . . for the powers of heaven shall
be shaken" (Luke 21:25, 26).

2. In the midst of this, the heavens open
and Jesus comes forth!

"And then shall appear the sign of the Son of man
in heaven; and then shall all the tribes
of the earth mourn, and they shall see the Son of man
coming in the clouds of heaven with power
and great glory" (Matt. 24:30).
". . . the Lord Jesus shall be revealed from heaven
with his mighty angels" (2 Thess. 1:7).
"Behold, he cometh with clouds; and every eye
shall see him . . ." (Rev. 1:7).
"And I saw heaven opened, and behold, a white
horse; and he that sat upon him was called
Faithful and True . . ." (Rev. 19:11).

3. The returning Savior touches down upon the

Mount of Olives, causing a great earthquake
(Zech. 14:4, 8).

Dr. J. Dwight Pentecost writes the following
concerning this earthquake:

"A news magazine reported some time ago that
a large hotel chain has sent a crew of engineers
and geologists to Jerusalem to explore the possibility
of building a hotel on the top of the Mount
of Olives. After their exploration they reported
that the site was a poor place to build because
the Mount of Olives is the center of a geological
fault, and an earthquake in that area might divide
the Mount and a hotel would certainly
be destroyed. So they decided against building there
and found another piece of property in another area.
Subsequently another hotel was erected
on the Mount of Olives which provides a breathtaking view of the old city of Jerusalem."[29]

4. After touching down on the Mount of Olives,
Christ proceeds to Petra and Bozrah, two chief
cities in Edom. While it is impossible to be
dogmatic here, it would seem that he goes to Edom
to gather the hiding Israelite remnant.
Accompanied by the holy angels, the church,
and the remnant, Christ marches toward
Armageddon (Isa. 34:6; 63:1).

B. The Purpose of the Second Coming of Christ

1. To defeat the antichrist and the world's nations
assembled at Armageddon.

---

[29]Pentecost, *Will Man Survive?*, p. 162.

Two authors aptly describe this battle for us:

"Palestine is to be given a blood bath of
unprecedented proportions, which will flow
from Armageddon at the north down through
the Valley of Jehoshaphat, will cover the land
of Edom, and will wash over all Judea and the city
of Jerusalem. John looks at this scene of carnage
and he describes it as blood flowing to the depths
of the horses' bridles. It is beyond human
imagination to see a lake that size that has been
drained from the veins of those who have followed
the purpose of Satan to try to exterminate God's
chosen people in order to prevent Jesus Christ
from coming to reign."[30]

"The Battle of Armageddon will result in wholesale
carnage among the legions of the beast. The
brilliance of Christ's appearing will produce a
trembling and demoralization in the soldiers
(Zech. 12:2; 14:13). The result of this demoralization and trembling will be the desertion from the
antichrist and the rendering of him inoperative
(2 Thess. 2:8). This tremendous light from heaven
will produce astonishment and blindness in animals
and madness in men (Zech. 12:4). A plague
will sweep through the armies from this light
and men will rot right where they stand
(Zech. 14:12, 15). The blood of animals
and men will form a lake two hundred miles long
and bridle deep (Rev. 14:19, 20). The stench
of this rotting mass of flesh and blood will fill the
entire region (Isa. 34:1-3). The mangled forms
of men and the rotting flesh of men and beasts
will provide a feast for the carrion birds

---

[30]Pentecost, *Prophecy for Today*, pp. 118, 119.

(Rev. 19:17, 18, 21). The beast and the false
prophet will then be cast alive into the lake
of fire forever (Rev. 19:20)."[31]

2. To regather, regenerate, and restore faithful
Israel.

Perhaps the most frequent promise in all the Old
Testament concerns God's eventual restoration
of Israel! The prophets repeat this so often
that it becomes a refrain — a chorus of confidence.

Note the following:

"Fear not, for I am with thee; I will bring thy seed
from the east, and gather thee from the west;
I will say to the north, Give up; and to the south,
Keep not back: bring my sons from far, and
my daughters from the ends of the earth"
(Isa. 43:5, 6).
"For I will set mine eyes upon them for good,
and I will bring them again to this land; and I will
build them, and not pull them down . . ."
(Jer. 24:6).
". . . Thus saith the Lord God, I will even gather you
from the people, and assemble you out of the
countries where ye have been scattered, and I
will give you the land of Israel" (Ezek. 11:17).
"And ye shall dwell in the land that I gave to
your fathers; and ye shall be my people,
and I will be your God" (Ezek. 36:28).
"And I will bring again the captivity of my people
of Israel, and they shall build the waste cities
and inhabit them; and they shall plant vineyards,
and drink the wine thereof; they shall also make

---

[31]Hoyt, *The End Times*, p. 165.

gardens, and eat the fruit of them. And I will plant
them upon their land, and they shall no more be
pulled up out of their land which I have given them,
saith the Lord thy God" (Amos 9:14, 15).

Perhaps the most sublime song of praise concerning
Israel's restoration is sung by the prophet Micah:

"Who is a God like unto thee, that pardoneth
iniquity, and passeth by the transgression
of the remnant of his heritage? He retaineth not
his anger for ever, because he delighteth in mercy.
He will turn again; he will have compassion
upon us; he will subdue our iniquities; and thou
wilt cast all their sins into the depths of the sea"
(Micah 7:18, 19).

In the New Testament our Lord also speaks
about this during one of his last sermons:

"And he shall send his angels with a great sound
of a trumpet, and they shall gather together his elect
from the four winds, from one end of heaven
to the other" (Matt. 24:31).

Thus will our Lord gather Israel when he comes
again and, as we have already observed, he will
begin by appearing to the remnant hiding in Edom.
Here we note:

   a. Their temporary sorrow.

   "And I will pour upon the house of David,
   and upon the inhabitants of Jerusalem,
   the spirit of grace and of supplications;
   and they shall look upon me whom
   they have pierced, and they shall mourn
   for him, as one mourneth for his only son,
   and shall be in bitterness for him,

as one that is in bitterness for his firstborn.
In that day shall there be a great mourning
in Jerusalem . . . in the valley of Megiddon.
And the land shall mourn, every family apart;
the family of the house of David apart,
and their wives apart . . ." (Zech. 12:10-12).
"And one shall say unto him, What are
these wounds in thine hands? Then he
shall answer, Those with which I was
wounded in the house of my friends"
(Zech. 13:6).
"Behold, he cometh with clouds; and every
eye shall see him, and they also which
pierced him; and all kindreds of the earth
shall wail because of him" (Rev. 1:7).

b.   Their ultimate joy.

"He will swallow up death in victory;
and the Lord God will wipe away tears
from off all faces; and the rebuke of his people
shall he take away from off all the earth;
for the Lord hath spoken it. And it shall
be said in that day, Lo, this is our God;
we have waited for him, and he will save us.
This is the Lord . . . we will be glad
and rejoice in his salvation" (Isa. 25:8, 9).
"Moreover, the light of the moon shall be
as the light of the sun, and the light of the sun
shall be sevenfold, as the light of seven days,
in the day that the Lord bindeth up
the breach of his people, and healeth
the stroke of their wound" (Isa. 30:26).
"He shall feed his flock like a shepherd;
he shall gather the lambs with his arm,
and carry them in his bosom, and shall gently

lead those that are with young" (Isa. 40:11).
"I, even I, am he that blotteth out thy
transgressions for mine own sake, and will not
remember thy sins" (Isa. 43:25).
"Can a woman forget her sucking child,
that she should not have compassion on the
son of her womb? Yea, they may forget,
yet will I not forget thee" (Isa. 49:15).
"For the Lord shall comfort Zion; he will
comfort all her waste places, and will make her
wilderness like Eden, and her desert like
the garden of the Lord; joy and gladness
shall be found therein; thanksgiving,
and the voice of melody" (Isa. 51:3).
"For ye shall go out with joy, and be led
forth with peace: the mountains and the hills
shall break forth before you into singing,
and all the trees of the field shall clap
their hands" (Isa. 55:12).

3. To judge and punish faithless Israel.

In the Book of Romans the great Apostle Paul
makes two significant statements concerning his
beloved nation Israel. He writes,

"And so all Israel shall be saved; as it is written,
There shall come out of Sion the Deliverer,
and shall turn away ungodliness from Jacob"
(Rom. 11:26).
"For they are not all Israel which are of Israel"
(Rom. 9:6).

By the first statement Paul of course meant that all
faithful Israel would be saved. As we have
previously seen, this blessed event will occur
during the Tribulation.

By the second statement Paul writes concerning
faithless Israel. In other words, all that glitters
is not gold! From the very moment God began
working through Abraham (the first Hebrew),
Satan also began working through members of that
same race. Thus, as the Bible has been advanced
by faithful Israel throughout history, it has
likewise been opposed by faithless Israel!

Therefore, when the master of all Israel returns,
he will be especially gracious to *true* Israel
but especially harsh with *false* Israel! Note
the tragic record of false Israel.

    a. Her sins against the Father

        (1) Rebelling (Num. 14:22, 23)
        (2) Rejecting (1 Sam. 8:7)
        (3) Robbing (Mal. 3:2-5)

    b. Her sins against the Son

        (1) She refused him (John 1:11).
        (2) She crucified him (Acts 2:22, 23;
        3:14, 15; 4:10; 5:30; 1 Thess. 2:14-16).

    c. Her sins against the Holy Spirit —
stubborn resistance! See Acts 7:51.

    d. Her sins against the kingdom

        (1) She refused to use her God-given
abilities to promote it (Luke 19:20-24;
Matt. 25:24-30).
        (2) She made light of the marriage
feast (Matt. 22:5).
        (3) She refused to wear the proper
wedding garments (Matt. 22:11-13).

e. Her sins against her own people

(1) She stole from widows (Matt. 23:14).

(2) She killed her own prophets (Matt. 23:31, 34, 35; Acts 7:58).

f. Her sins against the world

(1) She led others into her own wretched blindness (Matt. 23:16, 24).

(2) She was filled with hypocrisy (Matt. 16:6, 12; Rom. 2:17-23).

(3) She had blasphemed the name of God among the Gentiles (Rom. 2:24).

g. Her sins against the gospel

(1) She opposed it in Jerusalem (Acts 4:2; 5:28; 9:29; 21:28; 23:2, 12).

(2) She opposed it in Damascus (Acts 9:22-25).

(3) She opposed it in Antioch of Pisidia (Acts 13:45, 50).

(4) She opposed it in Iconium (Acts 14:2).

(5) She opposed it in Lystra (Acts 14:19).

(6) She opposed it in Thessalonica (Acts 17:5).

(7) She opposed it in Berea (Acts 17:13).

(8) She opposed it in Corinth (Acts 18:6, 12).

(9) She opposed it in Caesarea (Acts 25:6, 7).

The Apostle Paul dearly loved his nation, and doubtless wrote the following description of

faithless Israel and her future judgment with a
heavy and weeping heart:

"Who both killed the Lord Jesus, and their own
prophets, and have persecuted us; and they please
not God, and are contrary to all men, forbidding us
to speak to the Gentiles that they might be saved,
to fill up their sins alway: for the wrath is come
upon them to the uttermost" (1 Thess. 2:15, 16).

Thus the tragic prophecy of Ezekiel will someday
be fulfilled upon faithless Israel:

"But as for them whose heart walketh after the heart
of their detestable things and their abominations,
I will recompense their way upon their own
heads, saith the Lord God" (Ezek. 11:21).
"And I will purge out from among you the rebels,
and them that transgress against me . . ."
(Ezek. 20:38).

4. To separate the sheep from the goats.

"When the Son of man shall come in his glory,
and all the holy angels with him, then shall he sit
upon the throne of his glory. And before him
shall be gathered all nations; and he shall separate
them one from another, as a shepherd divideth
his sheep from the goats. And he shall set the sheep
on his right hand, but the goats on the left.
Then shall the King say unto them on his right hand,
Come, ye blessed of my Father, inherit the kingdom
prepared for you from the foundation of the world;
for I was hungry, and ye gave me food;
I was thirsty, and ye gave me drink; I was
a stranger, and ye took me in; naked and ye
clothed me; I was sick, and ye visited me; I was
in prison, and ye came unto me.

"Then shall the righteous answer him, saying,
Lord, when saw we thee hungry, and fed thee;
or thirsty, and gave thee drink? When saw we thee
a stranger, and took thee in; or naked, and
clothed thee? Or when saw we thee sick, or in prison,
and came unto thee?

"And the King shall answer and say unto them,
Verily I say unto you, Inasmuch as ye have done it
unto one of the least of these my brethren,
ye have done it unto me.

"Then shall he say also unto them on the left hand,
Depart from me, ye cursed, into everlasting fire,
prepared for the devil and his angels; for I was
hungry, and ye gave me no food; I was thirsty,
and ye gave me no drink; I was a stranger,
and ye took me not in; naked, and ye clothed
me not; sick, and in prison, and ye visited me not.

"Then shall they also answer him, saying, Lord,
when saw we thee hungry, or athirst, or a stranger,
or naked, or sick, or in prison, and did not
minister unto thee?

"Then shall he answer them, saying, Verily I say
unto you, Inasmuch as ye did it not to one of the least
of these, ye did it not to me.

"And these shall go away into everlasting punish-
ment, but the righteous into life eternal"
(Matt. 25:31-46).

    a. The false views of this judgment

        (1) That this "sheep and goat"
        judgment is the same as the great white
        throne judgment of Revelation 20:11-15.
        They are not the same, for one takes

place at the end of the Tribulation
while the other occurs at the end
of the millennium.
(2) That the sheep and goat judgment
deals only with entire nations.
Some have imagined the nations
of the world lined up before God. At his
command, Russia steps forward and
is judged — then America, then Cuba,
etc. This is not the case. The word
translated "nations" in Matthew 25:32
should be rendered "Gentiles."

b. The basis of this judgment

The test in this judgment is how those Gentiles
who survive the Tribulation have treated
faithful Israel (here referred to by Christ
as "my brethren").

In Nazi Germany, during the Second World
War, escaping Jews were on a number
of occasions befriended and protected by
various German families who, in spite of their
nationality, did not agree with Adolf Hitler.
Apparently the same thing will happen
during the Tribulation. Gentiles from all
nations will hear the message of faithful Israel
and believe it and, at the risk of their
own lives, will protect the messengers!

This, then, would seem to be the nature
of the sheep and goat judgment. See also
Matthew 13:38-43, 47-50; Genesis 12:1-3.

5. To bind Satan

"And the God of peace shall bruise Satan

under your feet shortly . . ." (Rom. 16:20).
"And I saw an angel come down from heaven,
having the key of the bottomless pit and a great
chain in his hand. And he laid hold on the dragon,
that old serpent, which is the Devil, and Satan,
and bound him a thousand years, and cast him
into the bottomless pit, and shut him up,
and set a seal upon him, that he should deceive
the nations no more till the thousand years should
be fulfilled . . ." (Rev. 20:1-3).

6. To resurrect Old Testament and tribulational
saints

It is the view of this study guide that at the
Rapture of the church God will raise only those believers who have been saved from Pentecost till the
Rapture. According to this view, all other believers
will be resurrected just prior to the millennium.

a. The fact of this resurrection.

At least nine passages bring out this
resurrection.

(1) Job 19:25, 26
"For I know that my redeemer liveth,
and that he shall stand at the latter day
upon the earth; and though after my skin
worms destroy this body, yet in my
flesh shall I see God."

(2) Psalm 49:15
"But God will redeem my soul from
the power of the grave, for he shall
receive me."

(3) Isaiah 25:8
"He will swallow up death in victory. . . ."

(4) Isaiah 26:19
"Thy dead men shall live; together
with my dead body shall they arise. . . ."
(5) Daniel 12:2
"And many of them that sleep in the dust
of the earth shall awake, some to
everlasting life, and some to shame
and everlasting contempt."
(6) Hosea 13:14
"I will ransom them from the power
of the grave; I will redeem them
from death: O death, I will be thy
plagues; O grave, I will be thy
destruction. . . ."
(7) John 5:28, 29
"Marvel not at this, for the hour is coming,
in the which all that are in the graves
shall hear his voice, and shall come forth;
they that have done good, unto
the resurrection of life; and they that
have done evil, unto the resurrection
of damnation."
(8) Hebrews 11:35
". . . and others were tortured, not
accepting deliverance, that they might
obtain a better resurrection."
(9) Revelation 20:4, 5
". . . and I saw the souls of them that
were beheaded for the witness of Jesus,
and for the Word of God, and which had
not worshipped the beast, neither
his image, neither had received his mark
upon their foreheads, or in their hands;
and they lived and reigned with Christ
a thousand years. But the rest of the dead

lived not again until the thousand
years were finished. . . ."

b. The order of this resurrection.

This is the third of four major biblical
resurrections. These are:

(1) The resurrection of Christ
(1 Cor. 15:23);
(2) The resurrection of believers
at the Rapture (1 Thess. 4:16;
1 Cor. 15:51-53);
(3) The resurrection of Old Testament
and tribulational saints;
(4) The resurrection of the unsaved
(Rev. 20:5, 11-14).

Thus one of the reasons for the second coming
will be to resurrect those non-church-related saints.
For many long centuries Father Abraham has been
patiently awaiting that city "which hath foundations,
whose builder and maker is God" (Heb. 11:10);
God will not let him down!

7. To judge fallen angels

"Know ye not that we shall judge angels?"
(1 Cor. 6:3).

All fallen angels are of course included in this
judgment. But some believe that they fall
into two main catagories — chained and unchained.

a. Unchained fallen angels

"And Jesus asked him, saying, What is thy
name? And he said, Legion, because
many devils were entered into him. And they

besought him that he would not command
them to go out into the deep" (Luke 8:30, 31).
"And there was in their synagogue a man
with an unclean spirit; and he cried out,
saying, Let us alone; what have we to do
with thee, thou Jesus of Nazareth? Art thou
come to destroy us? I know thee who
thou art, the Holy One of God"
(Mark 1:23, 24).
"For we wrestle not against flesh and blood,
but against principalities, against powers,
against the rulers of the darkness of this world,
against spiritual wickedness in high places"
(Eph. 6:12).

The point of these three passages is simply
this — there is a group of fallen angels
(demons) who have freedom of movement,
and can therefore possess the bodies
of both men and animals. Their one sin
was that of following Satan in his foul rebellion
against God. See Isaiah 14:12-17; Ezekiel
28:12-19.

b. Chained fallen angels

"Christ also suffered. He died once for the sins
of all us guilty sinners, although he himself
was innocent of any sin at any time,
that he might bring us safely home to God.
But though his body died, his spirit lived on,
and it was in the spirit that he visited
the spirits in prison, and preached to them —
spirits of those who, long before in the days
of Noah, had refused to listen to God,
though he waited patiently for them while
Noah was building the ark. Yet only eight

persons were saved from drowning in that
terrible flood" (1 Peter 3:18-20, TLB).
"For . . . God spared not the angels that sinned,
but cast them down to hell, and delivered
them into chains of darkness, to be reserved
unto judgment" (2 Peter 2:4).
"And the angels which kept not their first
estate, but left their own habitation,
he hath reserved in everlasting chains under
darkness unto the judgment of the great day"
(Jude 6).

According to the above passages these fallen
angels do not have the freedom the previous
angels do, but are right now in "solitary
confinement" awaiting their judgment
at the end of the Tribulation. Why the
difference? Many Bible scholars believe that
this group of angels was guilty of *two*
grievous sins — not only did they join Satan's
revolt, but they also committed sexual
perversion with "the daughters of men" before
the flood. See Genesis 6:2.

C. The Time-Element Involved in the Second Coming of Christ

According to Daniel 12:11, 12, there will be a period
of seventy-five days between the second coming of Christ
and the millennial reign. Dr. S. Franklin Logsdon
has written,

"We in the United States have a national analogy.
The President is elected in the early part of November,
but he is not inaugurated until January 20th. There is
an interim of 70-plus days. During this time,

he concerns himself with the appointment of Cabinet members, foreign envoys and others who will comprise his government. In the period of 75 days between the termination of the Great Tribulation and the Coronation, the King of glory likewise will attend to certain matters."[32]

It would therefore appear that the seventy-five days will be spent in accomplishing seven basic things already mentioned under "Purposes of the Second Coming."

---

[32]Logsdon, *Profiles of Prophecy,* p. 81.

VII. THE MILLENNIUM–
THE THOUSAND-YEAR
REIGN OF CHRIST

Some 250 years ago, Isaac Watts wrote a hymn
based on the truths found in Psalm 98. The name
of this world-famous hymn is *Joy to the World!*
At Christmas it is sung all across the world by millions
of Christians and non-Christians alike. But a close study
of the words of this hymn reveal that Watts did not have
in mind the *Bethlehem* coming of Christ, but rather
the *millennial* coming of our Lord! Observe his words:

> Joy to the world! The Lord is come!
> Let earth receive her King.
> Let every heart prepare him room,
> And heaven and nature sing.
> No more let sins and sorrows grow,
> Nor thorns infest the ground;
> He comes to make his blessings flow,
> Far as the curse is found.
> He rules the world with truth and grace,
> And makes the nations prove
> The glories of his righteousness,
> And wonders of his love.

A. The Fact of the Millennium

The word itself is a Latin term which signifies
"one thousand years."

". . . and they lived and reigned with Christ a
thousand years" (Rev. 20:4).

In the first seven verses of Revelation 20, John mentions
the thousand-year period no less than six times!
In spite of this some have argued that, since this number

is found in only one New Testament passage, one
cannot insist that the thousand-year period will really
come to pass! To emphasize their point, reference
is made to 2 Peter 3:8 — ". . . One day is with the Lord
as a thousand years, and a thousand years as one day."

It is interesting (and perhaps revealing) to note
that the same group which attempts to shorten
the thousand-year period of Revelation to one day
(and thus do away entirely with the millennium)
also attempts to expand the six days of creation in Genesis
to thousands of years! One is tempted to ask,
"Why can't God mean exactly what he says?"

Dr. Rene Pache writes the following helpful words:

"Let us notice again this fact: the teaching of the
Old Testament concerning the millennium is so complete
that the Jews in the Talmud succeeded in developing it
entirely themselves, without possessing the gifts furnished
later by the New Testament. For example, they had
indeed affirmed before the Apocalypse that the messianic
kingdom would last one thousand years. One should not,
therefore, claim (as some have done) that without
the famous passage of Revelation 20:1-10 the doctrine
of the millennium would not exist."[33]

During the history of the Christian church men have
held three major views about the millennium.

1. Postmillennialism

This theory says that through the preaching
of the gospel the world will eventually embrace
Christianity and become a universal "society
of saints." At this point Christ will be invited to
assume command and reign over man's peaceful

---

[33]Pache, *The Return of Jesus Christ*, p. 380.

planet. Thus, though postmillennialists believe
in a literal thousand-year reign, their position
is false, for the Bible clearly teaches that the world
situation will become worse and worse prior to
Christ's second coming — not better and better!
See 1 Timothy 4:1; 2 Tim. 3:1-5. This position
was popularized by a Unitarian minister named
Daniel Whitby (1638-1726), and it flourished
until the early part of the twentieth century.
Then came World War I, and men began to wonder.
Finally the postmillennial theory was quietly laid
to rest amid Hitler's gas ovens during
the Second World War! Today a postmillennialist
is harder to find than a 1940 Wendell Wilkie button!

2. Amillennialism

This view teaches that there will be no thousand-year
reign at all, and that the New Testament church
inherits all the spiritual promises and prophecies
of Old Testament Israel. In this view Isaiah's
beautiful prophecy of the bear and the cow
lying together and the lion eating straw like the ox
(Isa. 11:7) simply doesn't mean what it says
at all! However, if the eleventh chapter of Isaiah
cannot be taken literally, what proof do
we have that the magnificent fifty-third chapter
should not likewise be allegorized away?

3. Premillennialism

This view teaches that Christ will return just prior
to the millennium and will personally rule
during this glorious thousand-year reign.
This position alone is the scriptural one, and is
the oldest of these three views. From the
apostolic period on, the premillennial position
was held by the early church fathers.

a. Theologians who held it during the first
century A.D.

    (1) Clement of Rome — 40 to 100

    (2) Ignatius — 50-115

    (3) Polycarp — 70-167

b. Theologians who held it during the second
century A.D.

    (1) Justin Martyr — 100-168

    (2) Irenaeus — 140-202

    (3) Tertullian — 150-220

c. Theologians who held it during the third
century A.D.

    (1) Cyprian — 200-258

    (2) Commodianus — 250

Beginning in the fourth century, however, the
Roman Catholic Church began to grow and
premillennialism began to wither, for Rome
viewed herself as God's instrument to usher
in the promised kingdom of glory. For centuries
the precious doctrine of premillennialism was lost
except to a few groups.

But in the past few hundred years God has
graciously revived premillennialism and restored it
to its proper place, using men like Alford,
Seiss, Darby, and C. I. Scofield.

B. *The Purpose of the Millennium*

1. To reward the saints of God

"Verily there is a reward for the righteous . . ."
(Psa. 58:11).

"Behold, the Lord God will come with strong hand,
and his arm shall rule for him; behold,
his reward is with him . . ." (Isa. 40:10).
". . . to him that soweth righteousness shall be
a sure reward" (Prov. 11:18).
"Rejoice, and be exceeding glad, for great is
your reward in heaven . . ." (Matt. 5:12).
"For the Son of man shall come in the glory
of his Father with his angels; and then he shall
reward every man according to his works"
(Matt. 16:27).
"Knowing that of the Lord ye shall receive
the reward of the inheritance . . ." (Col. 3:24).
"And, behold, I come quickly, and my reward is
with me . . ." (Rev. 22:12).
"Then shall the King say . . . Come, ye blessed
of my Father, inherit the kingdom prepared for you
from the foundation of the world" (Matt. 25:34).

2. To answer the oft-prayed model prayer

In Luke 11:1-4 and Matthew 6:9-13 our Lord,
at the request of his disciples, suggested
a pattern prayer to aid all believers in their praying.
One of the guidelines was this: "Thy kingdom come!"
Here the Savior was inviting his followers
to pray for the millennium! Someday he will
return to fulfill the untold millions of times
these three little words have wafted their way
to heaven by Christians — "Thy kingdom come"!

3. To redeem creation

In Genesis 3 God cursed nature because
of Adam's sin. From that point on, man's paradise
became a wilderness. The roses suddenly
contained thorns, and the docile tiger became

a hungry meat eater! But during the millennium
all this will change. Paul describes the
transformation for us in his Epistle to the Romans:

"For all creation is waiting patiently and hopefully
for that future day when God will resurrect
his children. For on that day thorns and thistles,
sin, death, and decay — the things that overcame
the world against its will at God's command
— will all disappear, and the world around us
will share in the glorious freedom from sin which
God's children enjoy.

"For we know that even the things of nature,
like animals and plants, suffer in sickness
and death as they await this great event"
(Rom. 8:19-22, TLB).

4. To fulfill three important Old Testament
covenants

    a. The Abrahamic Covenant

God promised Abraham two basic things:

        (1) That his seed (Israel) would
        become a mighty nation (Gen. 12:1-3;
        13:16; 15:5; 17:7; 22:17, 18).
        (2) That his seed (Israel) would
        someday own Palestine forever
        (Gen. 12:7; 13:14, 15, 17; 15:7, 18-21;
        17:8).

    b. The Davidic Covenant (2 Chron. 13:5;
2 Sam. 7:12-16; 23:5)

Here the promise was threefold:

        (1) That from David would come an
        everlasting throne;

(2) That from David would come
an everlasting kingdom;
(3) That from David would come an
everlasting King.

c. The New Covenant (Jer. 31:31-34;
Isa. 42:6; Heb. 8:7-12)

This promise was also threefold:

(1) That he would forgive their iniquity
and forget their sin;
(2) That he would give them new
hearts;
(3) That he would use Israel to reach
and teach the Gentiles.

5. To complete a time-cycle (?)

A question mark is placed here because
this purpose is only a suggestion. However,
if one accepts the 4000 B.C. creation date of man,
and *if* the Rapture is truly near, then the millennium
will round out 7000 years of God's dealing
with mankind.

6. To prove a point

This is the point: regardless of his environment
or heredity, mankind apart from God's grace
will inevitably fail. For example:

a. The age of *Innocence* ended with
wilful disobedience (Gen. 3).

b. The age of *Conscience* ended with
universal corruption (Gen. 6).

c. The age of *Human Government* ended

206 THE KING IS COMING

with devil-worshiping at the Tower of Babel
(Gen. 11).

d. The age of *Promise* ended with God's
people out of the Promised Land and enslaved
in Egypt (Exod. 1).

e. The age of the *Law* ended with the creature
killing their Creator (Matt. 27).

f. The age of the *Church* will end
with worldwide apostasy (1 Tim. 4).

g. The age of the *Tribulation* will end
with the battle of Armageddon (Rev. 19).

h. The age of the *Millennium* will end
with an attempt to destroy God himself
(Rev. 20).

(Note — Just where and how Satan will gather
this unsaved human army at the end of the
millennium will be discussed later.)

7. To fulfill the main burden of biblical prophecy

All Bible prophecy concerning the Lord Jesus Christ
is summarized in one tiny verse by the Apostle
Peter — ". . . the sufferings of Christ, and the glory
that should follow" (1 Pet. 1:11).

Here Peter connects Christ's first coming
(the sufferings) with his second coming (the glory).
This in a nutshell is a panorama of the purpose,
plan, and program of Almighty Jehovah God!
Note this beautiful outline as we trace it
through the Word of God:

a. The *sufferings* — A Baby, wrapped in

swaddling clothes (Luke 2:12).
The *glory* — A King, clothed in majestic
apparel (Psa. 93:1).

b. The *sufferings* — He was the wearied
traveler (John 4:6).
The *glory* — He will be the untiring God
(Isa. 40:28, 29).

c. The *sufferings* — He had nowhere
to lay his head (Luke 9:58).
The *glory* — He will become heir to all things
(Heb. 1:2).

d. The *sufferings* — He was rejected
by tiny Israel (John 1:11).
The *glory* — He will be accepted by all
the nations (Isa. 9:6).

e. The *sufferings* — Wicked men took up
stones to throw at him (John 8:59).
The *glory* — Wicked men will cry for stones
to fall upon them to hide them from him
(Rev. 6:16).

f. The *sufferings* — A lowly Savior,
acquainted with grief (Isa. 53:3).
The *glory* — The mighty God, anointed
with the oil of gladness (Heb. 1:9).

g. The *sufferings* — He was clothed with a
scarlet robe in mockery (Luke 23:11).
The *glory* — He will be clothed with a vesture
dipped in the blood of his enemies
(Rev. 19:13).

h. The *sufferings* — He was smitten with
a reed (Matt. 27:30).

The *glory* — He will rule the nations with a rod of iron (Rev. 19:15).

i. *The sufferings* — Wicked soldiers bowed their knee and mocked (Mark 15:19).
The *glory* — Every knee shall bow and acknowledge Him (Phil. 2:10).

j. The *sufferings* — He wore the crown of thorns (John 19:5).
The *glory* — He will wear the crown of gold (Rev. 14:14).

k. The *sufferings* — His hands were pierced with nails (John 20:25).
The *glory* — His hands will carry a sharp sickle (Rev. 14:14).

l. The *sufferings* — His feet were pierced with nails (Psa. 22:16).
The *glory* — His feet will stand on the Mount of Olives (Zech. 14:4).

m. The *sufferings* — He had no form or comeliness (Isa. 53:2).
The *glory* — He will be the fairest of ten thousand (Psa. 27:4).

n. The *sufferings* — He delivered up his spirit (John 19:30).
The *glory* — He is alive forevermore (Rev. 1:18).

o. The *sufferings* — He was laid in the tomb (Matt. 27:59, 60).
The *glory* — He will sit on his throne (Heb. 8:1).

Here, then, is the "suffering-glory story" of the
Savior! Furthermore, when a sinner repents and
becomes a part of the Body of Christ, he too shares
in this destiny. Note the following:

"For I reckon that the sufferings of this present time
are not worthy to be compared with the glory
which shall be revealed in us" (Rom. 8:18).
"And our hope of you is steadfast, knowing that
as ye are partakers of the sufferings, so shall ye be
also of the consolation" (2 Cor. 1:7).
"If we suffer, we shall also reign with him . . ."
(2 Tim. 2:12).
"Beloved, think it not strange concerning the fiery
trial which is to try you, as though some strange
thing happened unto you; but rejoice, inasmuch
as ye are partakers of Christ's sufferings; that
when his glory shall be revealed, ye may be glad
also with exceeding joy" (1 Peter 4:12, 13).
"The elders which are among you I exhort, who
am also an elder, and a witness of the sufferings
of Christ, and also a partaker of the glory that
shall be revealed" (1 Peter 5:1).

C. *The Titles of the Millennium*

   1. The World to Come (Heb. 2:5)

   2. The Kingdom of Heaven (Matt. 5:10)

   3. The Kingdom of God (Mark 1:14)

   4. The Last Day (John 6:40)

   5. The Regeneration (Matt. 19:28)

"And Jesus said unto them, Verily I say unto you
that ye which have followed me, in the regeneration
when the Son of Man shall sit in the throne
of his glory, ye also shall sit upon twelve thrones
judging the twelve tribes of Israel" (Matt. 19:28).

The word "regeneration" is found only twice
in the English Bible, here and in Titus 3:5,
where Paul is speaking of the believer's new birth.
The word literally means "re-creation."
Thus the millennium will be to the earth
what salvation is to the sinner!

6. The Times of Refreshing (Acts 3:19)

7. The Restitution of All Things (Acts 3:21)

8. The Day of Christ. This is by far the most
common biblical name for the millennium.
See 1 Corinthians 1:8; 5:5; 2 Corinthians 1:14;
Philippians 1:6; 2:16.

D. Old Testament Examples of the Millennium

1. The Sabbath

This word literally means "rest." In Old Testament
times God wisely set aside a sabbath or rest time
after a period of activity.

A rest was to be observed —

a. After six workdays (Exod. 20:8-11;
Lev. 23:3);

b. After six work weeks (Lev. 23:15, 16);

    c. After six work months (Lev.
23:24, 25, 27, 34);

    d. After six work years (Lev. 25:2-5).

2. The Jubilee Year (Lev. 25:10-12)

3. The Tabernacle — because God's glory dwelt
in the Holy of Holies (Exod. 25:8; 29:42-46; 40:34)

4. The Feast of Tabernacles (Lev. 23:34-42)

5. The Promised Land (Deut. 6:3; Heb. 4:8-10)

6. The Reign of Solomon

    a. Because of the vastness of his kingdom
(1 Kings 4:21).

    b. Because of its security (1 Kings 4:25).

    c. Because of his great wisdom
(1 Kings 4:29, 34).

    d. Because of the fame of his kingdom
(1 Kings 10:7).

    e. Because of the riches of his kingdom
(1 Kings 10:27).

E. The Nature of the Millennium

What will the thousand-year reign of Christ be like?
Dr. J. Dwight Pentecost has compiled the following
extended and impressive facts:

> "A. Peace. The cessation of war through
> the unification of the kingdoms of the world

under the reign of Christ, together with the resultant
economic prosperity (since nations need not
devote vast proportions of their expenditure
on munitions) is a major theme of the prophets.
National and individual peace is the fruit
of Messiah's reign (Isa. 2:4; 9:4-7; 11:6-9; 32:17,
18; 33:5, 6; 54:13; 55:12; 60:18; 65:25; 66:12;
Ezek. 28:26; 34:25, 28; Hos. 2:18; Mic. 4:2, 3;
Zech. 9:10).

B. Joy. The fulness of joy will be a distinctive
mark of the age (Isa. 9:3, 4; 12:3-6; 14:7, 8;
25:8, 9; 30:29; 42:1, 10-12; 52:9; 60:15;
61:7, 10; 65:18, 19; 66:10-14; Jer. 30:18, 19;
31:13, 14; Zeph. 3:14-17; Zech. 8:18, 19; 10:6, 7).

C. Holiness. The theocratic kingdom will be
a holy kingdom, in which holiness is manifested
through the King and the King's subjects.
The land will be holy, the city holy, the temple holy,
and the subjects holy unto the Lord (Isa. 1:26, 27;
4:3, 4; 29:18-23; 31:6, 7; 35:8, 9; 52:1; 60:21;
61:10; Jer. 31:23; Ezek. 36:24-31; 37:23, 24;
43:7-12; 45:1; Joel 3:21; Zeph. 3:11, 13;
Zech. 8:3; 13:1, 2; 14:20, 21).

D. Glory. The kingdom will be a glorious kingdom,
in which the glory of God will find full manifestation
(Isa. 24:23; 4:2; 35:2; 40:5; 60:1-9).

E. Comfort. The King will personally minister
to every need, so that there will be the fulness
of comfort in that day (Isa. 12:1, 2; 29:22, 23;
30:26; 40:1, 2; 49:13; 51:3; 61:3-7;
66:13, 14; Jer. 31:23-25; Zeph. 3:18-20; Zech.
9:11, 12; Rev. 21:4).

F. Justice. There will be the administration
of perfect justice to every individual (Isa. 9:7;

11:5; 32:16; 42:1-4; 65:21-23; Jer. 23:5;
31:23; 31:29, 30).

G. Full knowledge. The ministry of the King
will bring the subjects of his kingdom into
full knowledge. Doubtless there will be an
unparalleled teaching ministry of the Holy Spirit
(Isa. 11:1, 2, 9; 41:19, 20; 54:13; Hab. 2:14).

H. Instruction. This knowledge will come
about through the instruction that issues from
the King (Isa. 2:2, 3; 12:3-6; 25:9; 29:17-24;
30:20, 21; 32:3, 4; 49:10; 52:8; Jer. 3:14, 15;
23:1-4; Mic. 4:2).

I. The removal of the curse. The original curse
placed upon creation (Gen. 3:17-19) will be
removed, so that there will be abundant
productivity to the earth. Animal creation will be
changed so as to lose its venom and ferocity
(Isa. 11:6-9; 35:9; 65:25).

J. Sickness removed. The ministry of the King
as a healer will be seen throughout the age,
so that sickness and even death, except as a penal
measure in dealing with overt sin, will be removed
(Isa. 33:24; Jer. 30:17; Ezek. 34:16).

K. Healing of the deformed. Accompanying
this ministry will be the healing of all deformity
at the inception of the millennium (Isa. 29:17-19;
35:3-6; 61:1, 2; Jer. 31:8; Mic. 4:6, 7;
Zeph. 3:19).

L. Protection. There will be a supernatural work
of preservation of life in the millennial age
through the King (Isa. 41:8-14; 62:8, 9;
Jer. 32:27; 23:6; Ezek. 34:27; Joel 3:16, 17;
Amos 9:15; Zech. 8:14, 15; 9:8; 14:10, 11).

M. Freedom from oppression. There will be
no social, political or religious oppression in that day

(Isa. 14:3-6; 42:6, 7; 49:8, 9; Zech. 9:11, 12).
N. No immaturity. The suggestion seems to be
that there will not be the tragedies of feeble-
mindedness nor of dwarfed bodies in that day
(Isa. 65:20). Longevity will be restored.
O. Reproduction by the living peoples.
The living saints who go into the millennium
in their natural bodies will beget children throughout
the age. The earth's population will soar.
These born in the age will not be born without a
sin nature, so salvation will be required (Jer. 30:20;
31:29; Ezek. 47:22; Zech. 10:8).
P. Labor. The period will not be characterized
by idleness, but there will be a perfect
economic system, in which the needs of men
are abundantly provided for by labor in that system,
under the guidance of the King. There will be
a fully developed industrialized society,
providing for the needs of the King's subjects
(Isa. 62:8, 9; 65:21-23; Jer. 31:5; Ezek.
48:18, 19). Agriculture as well as manufacturing
will provide employment.
Q. Economic prosperity. The perfect labor
situation will produce economic abundance,
so that there will be no want (Isa. 4:1; 35:1, 2, 7;
30:23-25; 62:8, 9; 65:21-23; Jer. 31:5, 12;
Ezek. 34:26; Mic. 4:1, 4; Zech. 8:11, 12; 9:16, 17;
Ezek. 36:29, 30; Joel 2:21-27; Amos 9:13, 14).
R. Increase of light. There will be an increase
of solar and lunar light in the age. This increased
light probably is a major cause in the increased
productivity of the earth (Isa. 4:5; 30:26;
60:19, 20; Zech. 2:5).
S. Unified language. The language barriers

will be removed so that there can be free social
interchange. (Zeph. 3:9).

T. Unified Worship. All the world will unite
in the worship of God and God's Messiah
(Isa. 45:23; 52:1, 7-10; 66:17-23; Zech. 13:2;
14:16; 8:23; 9:7; Zeph. 3:9; Mal. 1:11;
Rev. 5:9-14).

U. The manifest presence of God. God's presence
will be fully recognized and fellowship with God
will be experienced to an unprecedented degree
(Ezek. 37:27, 28; Zech. 2:2, 10-13; Rev. 21:3).

V. The fullness of the Spirit. Divine presence
and enablement will be the experience of all
who are in subjection to the authority of the King
(Isa. 32:13-15; 41:1; 44:3; 59:19, 21; 61:1;
Ezek. 36:26, 27; 37:14; 39:29; Joel 2:28, 29;
Ezek. 11:19, 20).

W. The perpetuity of the millennial state.
That which characterizes the millennial age is
not viewed as temporary, but eternal (Joel 3:20;
Amos 9:15; Ezek. 37:26-28; Isa. 51:6-8;
55:3, 13; 56:5; 60:19, 20; 61:8; Jer. 32:40;
Ezek. 16:60; 43:7-9; Dan. 9:24; Hos. 2:19-23)."[34]

F. The Citizens of the Millenium

1. Considered Negatively

No unsaved persons will enter the millennium
(John 3:3; Matt. 18:3; Jer. 31:33, 34; Ezek.
20:37, 38; Zech. 13:9; Matt. 25:30, 46;
Isa. 35). However, millions of babies will evidently
be reared in the millennium. They will be born

---

[34]Pentecost, *Things to Come*, pp. 487-490.

of saved but mortal Israelite and Gentile parents
who survived the Tribulation and entered
the millennium in that state of mortality (thus
the possible reason for the Tree of Life in Revelation
22:2). As they mature, some of these babies
will refuse to submit their hearts to the new birth,
though their outward acts will be subjected to
existing authority. Thus Christ will rule
with a rod of iron (Rev. 2:27; 12:5; 19:15;
Zech. 14:17-19).

Dr. Rene Pache writes concerning this:

"As beautiful as the Millennium is, it will not be
heaven. . . . Sin will still be possible during the
thousand years (Isa. 11:4; 65:20). Certain families
and certain nations will refuse to go up to Jerusalem
to worship the Lord (Zech. 14:17-19).
Such deeds will be all the more inexcusable
because the tempter will be absent and because
the revelations of the Lord will be greater. . . .
Those who have been thus smitten will serve
as examples to all those who would be tempted
to imitate them (Isa. 66:24)."[35]

2. Considered Positively

    a. Saved Israel

        (1) Israel will once again be related
        to God by marriage (Isa. 54:1-17;
        62:2-5; Hos. 2:14-23).
        (2) Israel will be exalted above
        the Gentiles (Isa. 14:1, 2; 49:22, 23;
        60:14-17; 61:6, 7).
        (3) Israel will become God's witness

---

[35]Pache, *The Return of Jesus Christ,* pp. 428, 429.

during the millennium (Isa. 44:8;
61:6; 66:21; Jer. 16:19-21; Mic. 5:7;
Zeph. 3:20; Zech. 4:1-7; 8:3).

b. Saved Old Testament and tribulation
Gentiles (Rev. 5:9, 10; Isa. 2:4; 11:12)

c. The church (1 Cor. 6:2; Rev. 1:6;
2:26, 27; 3:21; 2 Tim. 2:12)

d. The elect angels (Heb. 12:22)

G. *The King of the Millennium*

The Lord Jesus Christ will of course be King supreme,
but there are passages which suggest that he will graciously
choose to rule through a vice-regent, and that vice-
regent will be David! Note the following Scripture:

"But they shall serve the Lord their God, and David
their king, whom I will raise up unto them"
(Jer. 30:9).

Jeremiah wrote these words some 400 years after the
death of David, so he could not have been referring
to his earthly reign here.

"And I will set up one shepherd over them, and he
shall feed them, even my servant David; he shall feed
them, and he shall be their shepherd" (Ezek. 34:23).
See also Ezekiel 37:24.

"Afterward shall the children of Israel return,
and seek the Lord their God, and David their king,
and shall fear the Lord and his goodness in the latter days"
(Hos. 3:5).

If we can take these passages literally, David will once
again sit upon the throne of Israel. He will thus

be aided in his rule by —

1. The church (1 Cor. 6:3);
2. The apostles (Matt. 19:28);
3. Nobles (Jer. 30:21);
4. Princes (Isa. 32:1; Ezek. 45:8, 9);
5. Judges (Zech. 3:7; Isa. 1:26).

H. The Geography of the Millennium

1. Palestine

    a. To be greatly enlarged and changed (Isa. 26:15; Obad. 1:17-21).

    For the first time Israel will possess all the land promised to Abraham in Genesis 15:18-21.

    b. A great fertile plain to replace the mountainous terrain.

    c. A river to flow east-west from the Mount of Olives into both the Mediterranean and the Dead Seas.

    The following passages from *The Living Bible* bear this out:

    ". . . The Mount of Olives will split apart, making a very wide valley running from east to west, for half the mountain will move toward the north and half toward the south. . . . "Life-giving waters will flow out from Jerusalem, half toward the Dead Sea and half toward the Mediterranean, flowing continuously both in winter and in summer. . . . "All the land from Geba (the northern

border of Judah) to Rimmon (the southern
border) will become one vast plain . . ."
(Zech. 14:4, 8, 10).

"Sweet wine will drip from the mountains,
and the hills shall flow with milk. Water
will fill the dry stream beds of Judah,
and a fountain will burst forth from the temple
of the Lord to water Acacia Valley"
(Joel 3:18).

"He told me: 'This river flows east through
the desert and the Jordan Valley to the
Dead Sea, where it will heal the salty waters
and make them fresh and pure. Everything
touching the water of this river shall live.
Fish will abound in the Dead Sea,
for its waters will be healed. . . .
"All kinds of fruit trees will grow along
the river banks. The leaves will never
turn brown and fall, and there will always
be fruit. There will be a new crop every
month — without fail! For they are watered
by the river flowing from the Temple.
The fruit will be for food and the leaves
for medicine" (Ezek. 47:8, 9, 12).

2. Jerusalem

   a. The city will become the worship center
   of the world.

   "But in the last days Mount Zion will be
   the most renowned of all the mountains
   of the world, praised by all nations; people
   from all over the world will make pilgrimages
   there" (Mic. 4:1).

"In the last days Jerusalem and the Temple
of the Lord will become the world's greatest
attraction, and people from many lands
will flow there to worship the Lord.
'Come,' everyone will say, 'let us go up
the mountain of the Lord, to the Temple
of the God of Israel; there he will teach us
his laws, and we will obey them. For in
those days the world will be ruled from
Jerusalem" (Isa. 2:2, 3).

b. The city will occupy an elevated site
(Zech. 14:10).

c. The city will be six miles in circumference
(Ezek. 48:35). (In the time of Christ
the city was about four miles.)

d. The city will be named "Jehovah-
Shammah," meaning "the Lord is there"
(Ezek. 48:35).

I. The Temple in the Millennium

1. Its biblical order

The millennial temple is the last of seven
great scriptural temples. These are:

a. The tabernacle of Moses — Exodus 40
(1500-1000 B.C.);

b. The temple of Solomon — 1 Kings 8
(1000-586 B.C.);

c. The temple of Zerubbabel (rebuilt later

by Herod) — Ezra 6; John 2 (516 B.C. to A.D. 70);

d. The temple of the Body of Jesus — John 2:21 (4 B.C. to A.D. 30);

e. The spiritual temple, the church — Acts 2; 1 Thess. 4 (from Pentecost till the Rapture)

    (1) The whole church (Eph. 2:21)
    (2) The local church (1 Cor. 3:16, 17)
    (3) The individual Christian (1 Cor. 6:19)

f. The tribulational temple — Revelation 11 (from the Rapture till Armageddon);

g. The millennial temple — Ezekiel 40—48; Joel 3:18; Isaiah 2:3; 60:13; Daniel 9:24; Haggai 2:7, 9.

2. Its Holy Oblation

Palestine will be redistributed among the twelve tribes of Israel during the millennium. The land itself will be divided into three areas. Seven tribes will occupy the northern area and five the southern ground. Between these two areas there is a section called "the holy oblation," that is, that portion of ground which is set apart for the Lord. Dr. J. Dwight Pentecost quotes Merrill F. Unger on this:

"The holy oblation would be a spacious square, thirty-four miles each way, containing about 1160 square miles. This area would be the center of all the interests of the divine government and worship as set up in the Millennial earth. . . . The temple itself would be located in the middle

of this square (the holy oblation) and not in
the City of Jerusalem, upon a very high mountain,
which will be miraculously made ready for that
purpose when the temple is to be erected
(see Isa. 2:4; Micah 4:1-4; Ezek. 37:26).[36]

3. Its priesthood

On four specific occasions we are told that
the sons of Zadok will be assigned the priestly
duties (Ezek. 40:46; 43:19; 44:15; 48:11).

Zadok was a high priest in David's time (the eleventh
in descent from Aaron). His loyalty to the King
was unwavering. Because of this, he was
promised that his seed would have this glorious
opportunity (1 Sam. 2:35; 1 Kings 2:27, 35).

4. Its prince

In his description of the temple, Ezekiel refers
to a mysterious "prince" some seventeen times.
Whoever he is, he occupies a very important role
in the temple itself, apparently holding an
intermediary place between the people and the
priesthood. We are sure that he is not Christ,
since he prepares a sin offering for himself
(Ezek. 45:22), and is married and has sons
(Ezek. 46:16). Some suggest that the prince
is from the seed of King David, and that he will be
to David what the false prophet was to the antichrist.

5. Its negative aspects

Several articles and objects present in the temples
of Moses, Solomon, and Herod will be absent
from the millennial temple.

---

[36]Pentecost, *Things to Come*, pp. 510, 514.

a. There will be no veil.
This was torn in two from top to bottom
(Matt. 27:51) and will not reappear in this
temple. Thus there will be no barrier to keep
man from the glory of God.

b. There will be no table of showbread.
This will not be needed, for the Living Bread
himself will be present.

c. There will be no lampstands.
These will not be needed either, since the
Light of the World himself will personally
shine forth.

d. There will be no ark of the Covenant.
This will also be unnecessary, since the
Shekinah Glory himself will hover over
all the world, as the glory cloud once did
over the ark.

e. The East Gate will be closed.
Observe the words of Ezekiel: "This gate
shall be shut, and no man shall enter in by it;
because the Lord, the God of Israel,
hath entered in by it; therefore it shall be shut"
(Ezek. 44:2). This gate, it has been suggested,
will remain closed for the following reasons:

> (1) This will be the gate by which
> the Lord Jesus Christ enters the temple.
> As a mark of honor to an eastern king,
> no person could enter the gate by
> which he entered.
> (2) It was from the eastern gate that
> the glory of God departed for the last time
> in the Old Testament (Ezek. 10:18, 19).

> By sealing the gate, God reminds
> all those within that his glory will
> never again depart from his people.

6. Its sacrifices

As we have already seen, several pieces
of furniture in the Old Testament temple will be
missing in the millennial edifice. However,
the brazen altar of sacrifice will again be present.
There are at least four Old Testament prophecies
which speak of animal sacrifices in the millennial
temple: Isaiah 56:6, 7; 60:7; Zechariah 14:16-21;
Jeremiah 33:18. But why the need of these
animal blood sacrifices during the golden age
of the millennium?

To answer this, one must attempt to project himself
into this fabulous future period. Here is an age
of no sin, sorrow, sufferings, sickness, Satan,
or separation. During the millennium even the
vocabulary will be different. For example,
today respectable and decent society shuns
certain filthy four-letter words, and well they should!
This will doubtless also be practiced during
the millennium, but how the words will change!
Below is a sampling of some four-letter "cuss words"
to be shunned during the thousand-year reign:

> *fear*
> *pain*
> *jail*
> *hate*
> *dope*

We wonder if anyone blushed or felt shocked
while reading these wicked words. Probably not!

They are so much a part of our sinful society
that it is utterly impossible to avoid or ignore them!
The point is simply this: during the millennium
millions of children will be born and reared
by saved Israelite and Gentile parents who
survived the Tribulation. In spite of their perfect
environment, however, these "kingdom kids"
will need the new birth. As sons and daughters
of Adam they, too, as all others, will require
eternal salvation (Rom. 3:23; John 3:3). But how
can these children be reached? What object
lessons can be used? Here is a generation
which will grow up without knowing fear,
experiencing pain, witnessing hatred, taking dope,
or seeing a jail!

This is one reason that the sacrificial system will be
reinstituted during the millennium. These
sacrifices will function as

    a. A reminder to all of the necessity of the
    new birth;
    b. An object lesson of the costliness of
    salvation;
    c. An example of the awfulness of sin;
    d. An illustration of the holiness of God.

VIII. THE FINAL REVOLT OF SATAN

"And when the thousand years are expired, Satan shall be loosed out of his prison, and shall go out to deceive the nations which are in the four quarters of the earth, Gog and Magog, to gather them together to battle, the number of whom is as the sand of the sea. And they went up on the breadth of the earth, and compassed the camp of the saints about, and the beloved city . . ." (Rev. 20:7-9).

Dr. J. Vernon McGee writes the following words concerning these verses:

"When the late Dr. Chafer (founder of Dallas Theological Seminary) was once asked why God loosed Satan after he once had him bound, he replied, 'If you will tell me why God let him loose in the first place, I will tell you why God lets him loose the second time.' Apparently Satan is released at the end of the Millennium to reveal that the ideal conditions of the kingdom, under the personal reign of Christ, do not change the human heart. This reveals the enormity of the enmity of man against God. Scripture is accurate when it describes the heart as 'desperately wicked' and incurably so. Man is totally depraved. The loosing of Satan at the end of the 1000 years proves it."[37]

We have already discussed the purposes accomplished by the sacrifices during the millennium. Apparently millions of maturing children will view these sacrifices and hear the tender salvation plea of the priests,

---

[37]McGee, *Reveling through Revelation*, pp. 74, 75.

but will stubbornly harden their sinful hearts. The fact
that earth's mighty King at Jerusalem once bled
as a lowly Lamb at Calvary will mean absolutely nothing
to them! Outwardly they will conform, but inwardly
they will despise.

Finally, at the end of the millennium, the world will be
offered for the first time in ten centuries "a choice,
and not an echo." Millions will make a foolish
and fatal choice!

Dr. J. Dwight Pentecost quotes F. C. Jennings,
who writes:

"Has human nature changed, at least apart from
sovereign grace? Is the carnal mind at last friendship
with God? Have a thousand years of absolute power and
absolute benevolence, both in unchecked activity,
done away with all war forever and forever?
These questions must be marked by a practical test.
Let Satan be loosed once more from his prison.
Let him range once more earth's smiling fields
that he knew of old. He saw them last soaked with blood
and flooded with tears, the evidence and accompaniments
of his own reign; he sees them now 'laughing
with abundance'. . . . But as he pursues his way
further from Jerusalem, the center of this blessedness,
these tokens become fainter, until, in the faroff
"corner of the earth," they cease altogether,
for he find myriads who have instinctively shrunk
from close contact with that holy center, and are not
unprepared once more to be deceived."[38]

However, this insane and immoral insurrection
is doomed to utter and complete failure. As a war

---

[38]Pentecost, *Things to Come*, p. 549.

correspondent, the Apostle John duly records this final battle:

". . . and fire came down from God out of heaven, and devoured them. And the devil that deceived them was cast into the lake of fire and brimstone, where the beast and the false prophet are, and shall be tormented day and night for ever and ever" (Rev. 20:9, 10).

Obviously this battle, referred to as Gog and Magog, is not the same as the one in Ezekiel 38 and 39. Dr. J. Vernon McGee writes concerning this:

"Because the rebellion is labeled 'Gog and Magog,' many Bible students identify it with Gog and Magog of Ezekiel 38 and 39. This, of course, is not possible, for the conflicts described are not parallel as to time, place, or participants — only the name is the same.

"The invasion from the north by Gog and Magog of Ezekiel 38 and 39 breaks the false peace of the Antichrist and causes him to show his hand in the midst of the Great Tribulation. That rebellion of the godless forces from the north will have made such an impression on mankind that after 1000 years the last rebellion of man bears the same label. We have passed through a similar situation in this century. World War I was so devastating that when war again broke out in Europe, it was labeled again "World War," but differentiated by the number 2. Now World War III is being predicted! Likewise the war in Ezekiel 38 and 39 is Gog and Magog I, while this reference in verse 8 is to Gog and Magog II."[39]

---

[39]McGee, *Reveling through Revelation*, p. 77.

IX. THE GREAT
WHITE THRONE JUDGMENT

A. The Fact of this Throne (Hebrews 9:27)

"And I saw a great white throne, and him that sat on it,
from whose face the earth and the heaven fled away;
and there was found no place for them. And I saw
the dead, small and great, stand before God;
and the books were opened; and another book
was opened, which is the book of life; and the dead
were judged out of those things which were written
in the books, according to their works. And the sea
gave up the dead which were in it; and death
and hell delivered up the dead which were in them;
and they were judged every man according to their works.
And death and hell were cast into the lake of fire.
This is the second death. And whosoever was not found
written in the book of life was cast into the lake of fire"
(Rev. 20:11-15).

"I behold till the thrones were cast down, and the Ancient
of Days did sit, whose garment was white as snow,
and the hair of his head like the pure wool;
his throne was like the fiery flame, and his wheels
as burning fire. A fiery stream issued and came forth
from before him; thousand thousands ministered unto him,
and ten thousand times ten thousand stood before him;
the judgment was set, and the books were opened"
(Dan. 7:9, 10).

B. The Judge of this Throne — Christ Himself!

"For the Father judgeth no man, but hath committed
all judgment unto the Son . . . and hath given him

authority to execute judgment also, because he is
the Son of man" (John 5:22, 27).
"Him God raised up the third day, and showed him
openly. . . . And he commanded us to preach unto
the people, and to testify that it is he which was ordained
of God to be the Judge of quick and dead"
(Acts 10:40, 42).
"I charge thee therefore before God, and the Lord
Jesus Christ, who shall judge the quick and the dead
at his appearing and his kingdom . . ." (2 Tim. 4:1).

C. The Jury at this Throne — Five Sets of Books

1. The book of conscience (Rom. 2:15)

Although man's conscience is not an infallible guide,
he will nevertheless be condemned by those
occasions when he deliberately violated it.

2. The book of words (Matt. 12:36, 37)

"But I say unto you that every idle word that men
shall speak, they shall give account thereof in the day
of judgment. For by thy words thou shalt
be justified, and by thy words thou shalt be
condemned."

3. The book of secret words

"God shall judge the secrets of men by Jesus Christ"
(Rom. 2:16).
"For God shall bring every work into judgment,
with every secret thing, whether it be good,
or whether it be evil" (Eccles. 12:14).

4. The book of public works

". . . whose end shall be according to their works"
(2 Cor. 11:15).
"For the Son of man shall come in the glory
of his Father with his angels; and then he shall
reward every man according to his works"
(Matt. 16:27).

5. The book of life (Exod. 32:32, 33; Psa. 69:28;
Dan. 12:1; Phil. 4:3; Rev. 3:5; 13:8; 17:8;
20:12, 15; 21:27; 22:19)

D. The Judged at this Throne

As has previously been discussed (see notes under
"The Judgment Seat of Christ"), only unsaved people
will stand before this throne.

"The wicked shall be turned into hell, and all the nations
that forget God" (Psa. 9:17).

E. The Judgment at this Throne —
The Eternal Lake of Fire
(Revelation 20:14, 15; Matthew 25:41, 46)

X. THE DESTRUCTION OF THIS PRESENT EARTH AND SURROUNDING HEAVENS

A. The Fact of this Destruction

"Heaven and earth shall pass away, but my words shall not pass away" (Matt. 24:35).

"Thou, Lord, in the beginning hast laid the foundation of the earth, and the heavens are the works of thine hands; they shall perish, but thou remainest; and they shall all wax old as doth a garment, and as a vesture shalt thou fold them up, and they shall be changed; but thou art the same, and thy years shall not fail" (Heb. 1:10-12).

"But the day of the Lord will come as a thief in the night, in the which the heavens shall pass away with a great noise, and the elements shall melt with fervent heat; the earth also and the works that are therein shall be burned up" (2 Peter 3:10, 11).

B. The Reason for this Destruction

At this stage in the Bible the final rebellion has been put down, the false prophet, the antichrist, and the Devil himself are all in the lake of fire forever, and the wicked dead have been judged. In light of this, why the necessity for this awesome destruction?

To help illustrate, consider the following: let us suppose that a flag-hating hippie breaks into the money vaults of Fort Knox, Kentucky and, to show his utter contempt for America's capitalistic system, begins pouring filthy crankcase oil on the stacked bars of gold and silver. Upon leaving however, he is caught, tried, and confined

to prison. The authorities thereupon close their books
on the Fort Knox case. But the gunk on the gold
remains! In this illustration, the vandal would represent
the Devil, the crankcase oil would stand for sin,
and the gold and silver for God's perfect creation.
God will someday arrest the Devil, of course, and forever
confine him to prison. But what about the oily
sin-stains that remain on his gold and silver creation?
To solve the problem, God does what the Fort Knox
authorities might consider doing — he purges the stains
in a fiery wash! And it works! For the hotter the flame,
the more rapidly the oil evaporates, and the brighter
the gold becomes!

God will someday do to creation what he did to his
beloved Israel in the Old Testament:

"Behold, I have refined thee . . . I have chosen thee
in the furnace of affliction" (Isa. 48:10).

XI. THE NEW CREATION OF HEAVEN AND EARTH

"For, behold, I create new heavens and a new earth;
and the former shall not be remembered, nor come
into mind" (Isa. 65:17).
"For as the new heavens and the new earth,
which I shall make, shall remain before me, saith the
Lord, so shall your seed and your name remain"
(Isa. 66:22).
"Nevertheless we, according to his promise, look for
new heavens and a new earth, wherein dwelleth
righteousness" (2 Peter 3:13).
"And I saw a new heaven and a new earth; for the
first heaven and the first earth were passed away;
and there was no more sea" (Rev. 21:1).

Some see this new world as the last of eight reshaped
worlds. These would include:

A. The original world (Gen. 1:1; Ezek. 28:13)
B. The ruined world (Gen. 1:2a)
C. The Remolded world (Gen. 1:2b—3:5)
D. The pre-flood world (Gen. 3:6—7:10)
E. The present world (Gen. 9:1-17; Rom. 8:19-22)
F. The tribulational world (Isa. 24; Rev. 6—19)
G. The millennial world (Isa. 35)
H. The new world (Rev. 21, 22)